1

I used to hate being named Aristotle McCreadie. I thought the name was tacky. But over the years I guess I've gotten accustomed to it. It was my dad's idea, and maybe a way of toughening me up, which didn't really work. But this isn't the story of How I Got My Name, and it's not a weepy memoir. It's about a time in my life not long ago when I was at my laziest. And that's saying something for me. But what made this lazy spell so different than my others is that I accidentally solved a murder and saved an entire town just by sitting around, drinking mai tais and being nosy.

I lived in Playa Santiago in the marina in a house boat. The place had a kitchen, a bathroom and a shower that was so small I had to stoop to stand in it. I slept most nights on the deck, with the boat creaking and swaying in the water and the waves rocking pleasantly as I slept. I didn't really have any plans for my future. I didn't know anyone in the town when I moved there. I told my mom I was retired and she said 30 was maybe a little early for that. But she didn't give me any grief about it. Maybe she knew I was going through a phase that was necessary for my development. The real reason I had gone to Playa Santiago might sound ridiculous, but if you've been there you'll understand. It was a tiki bar.

For tiki people, this was kind of like visiting the Wailing Wall. Except happier. Well, it's not a good metaphor, but it's a spiritual experience, okay? And before you judge me, hear me out for a minute.

The place I'm talking about, of course, is Pirate's Cove, which in many circles is considered the greatest tiki bar in the world. What makes a great tiki bar? I'll try to tell you, but I'm warning you that even spelling it out in some way cheapens the experience. It's like summarizing *War and Peace* to a 12-year-old in a text message. At some point the kid has to grow up and read the book for himself. You just need to go to Pirate's Cove. Not right now. You can wait until you finish this chapter to book your tickets. But I digress, and basically I'm stalling so I can think about this.

Okay, here are a few things: a great tiki bar first of all has to have an unreasonable, obsessive, totally unnecessary, maniacal, economically stupid fixation on the integrity of the ingredients. I'm not talking about the tropical themed restaurant next to the Jack in the Box in your hometown. The kind of bar I'm talking about is very, very rare. I'm talking about a bar where they grate fresh nutmeg into your drink. They use fresh passion fruit, which is flown in once a week from a farm in Ecuador that is located in the world's premium microclimate for growing said fruit. And the rum? They'll have a ridiculously huge variety of rums you've never heard of. Aged golden rums, white rums, spiced rums, black rums. And some of these rums are rare; so rare you can't even call them top shelf. You'll see a twenty-five year rum aged in sherry casks, bought from a guy who only makes a thousand bottles a year and sells to three bars in the world. And the thing about the Great Tiki Bar is that you'd have to ask the regulars if you wanted to know this stuff. They're not advertising this information.

And the recipes? Recipes that are only known by one person, the guy who invented the drink. And maybe his son. Secret syrups and spice mixtures, the ingredients of which are unknown to even bartenders themselves. These are recipes that have been handed down from several generations. They've been perfected, obsessed over, tweaked. These recipes are the subject of debates that can lead to fistfights. Tiki people have spent decades trying to learn these recipes. Some of these drinks started as mistakes when a bartender put two shots of spiced rum instead of tequila, and one shot of passion fruit instead of two. I'm talking about cocktails with stories, legends, creation myths. Am I taking this too far? Well, I'll have you know that I'm pretty mellow about this compared with some of the old timers I've met. I'm a pretty new student of this as a matter of fact. And I have a lot more to learn.

The décor? Waterfalls. Tropical fish. Vintage South Pacific travel posters. Giant, bulbous blowfish hanging from the ceiling. Old fishing gear. Nautical ropes hanging all over the…you know, I'm getting ahead of myself. I need to tell you about Pirate's Cove itself. Now, if you've been there, you can skip this part, or you can read it and write down the stuff I left out in the margins. Because I can't possibly give every detail. That summer was important for me, because I had never been to the Cove. I was in the infancy of my tiki interest, and the place was so legendary that something drew me there. I just *had to go.*

I was in town for a week before I worked up the guts to finally go in the place. I would walk down the beach and see it full of regulars and keep walking. But finally one afternoon I woke up on the boat after a nap and trudged down the beach the quarter mile past the bungalows and beach cottages, and the place was just opening up and I knew it was time for me. The old man was getting all his ingredients in order and washing glasses, and there was only one customer, and the stars were aligned, and I had to make my move. The sun was sinking into the golden glory of the post-four o'clock haze. To get into the Cove, you *have to walk on sand.* The entrance is on the beach itself. I love that.

So I just walked right in there and sat down. The bar is a strange old shack that seems half built out of bamboo and it only seems to have three walls. I honestly couldn't tell what they did when the place closed down at night, because the bar just opened out onto the sand and it was about fifty feet to the water. I sat at the bar and looked out at the beach, and an old boat was abandoned and half covered in sand, waves washing onto the old mossy wood. A couple of fishing boats were out there in the water and a warm breeze blew in from the ocean. A ceiling fan twirled above me. I counted five aquariums in the bar, and they were full of oddly shaped, colorful tropical fish. The nautical rope was hanging from the ceiling, and there were vintage Hawaiian travel posters, and paintings of volcanoes and little tiki statues and little mechanical waterfalls. The whole bar was *alive*.

The other customer was an over-tanned beach bum in shorts and a white button-down shirt that was splashed with paint. He was about fifty with thinning golden blonde hair, and he was in the middle of some discourse.

"Tom told me they refinanced the place five years ago anyway. And they brought my guys in there to fix the plumbing stuff last year, and that was a hell of a job. And he told me the realtor said they could get a million five for it. Shit. A million five. The market is crazy right now. Imagine how much this place could go for. You could probably get two million for it. Sell it to some assholes from LA."

He took a sip of a large blue cocktail that was garnished with an orange slice and a flower and served in a hurricane glass.

"So what did he tell you about Sam? Do they know anything yet?"

The bartender shook his head sadly. "I'll tell you in a second."

He walked over to me and placed a napkin on the bar in front of me. He gave the nod of a truly relaxed neighborhood bartender. There was no "How can I help you?" It was just a nod.

"Mai tai," I said, my voice cracking with nervousness. Goddamn it. I was trying so hard to sound mellow. He smiled as if to say "Good choice, my friend." I tried to watch him make it but his hands were flying so fast under the bar and I didn't want to look like I was spying, so I casually looked out at the beach a few times. He took a cocktail shaker off of a rickety old shelf behind him, filled it with about seven different spirits and syrups from various unlabelled bottles, his hands working like a magician.

Then he filled it with ice, that wonderful *slushing* sound, and covered it, and then came the shake. He shook it almost as a meditative activity. It was fast, and he shook it horizontally at eye level, and his eyes closed slightly, and he shook it *forever*. When he finished, he took an old fashioned glass off of another shelf, filled it with ice, and then poured the yellow-pink mixture into the ice. He floated a little bit of dark rum on top. Then he garnished the drink with a pink flower, a maraschino cherry, and my favorite thing to watch, the carving of the orange peel. He took the orange peel and placed it gingerly on top in an unbelievable upside down "Q" shape, put the straw inside, and placed it on my napkin with a little sparkle in his eyes. He had gray hair and he must've been around sixty years old.

I sipped it, staring out at the beach. It was clearly a mai tai – it had the orange liqueur and the almond syrup, the fresh sourness of the lime, and the mixture of light and dark rums – but there were other flavors in there, layers of complexity that shocked my palate at first. I was getting hints of herbal bitterness here, hints of smoke on the finish, and an absolutely muted element of sweetness. My God, I thought. This is a real cocktail.

I almost wept; I'd been waiting years to come here and taste this thing. I looked at the menu sitting on the bar near me. The menu was enormous, and I had never heard of most of these drinks. This was a university, a library, a living museum of cocktails. I was still marveling over my drink when they continued their conversation. I overheard, mildly interested.

"So," the bartender told the regular. "Tom told me that whoever did it knew everything about the house."

"What? Knew everything?"

"They knew how to disable the alarm system. They cleaned up after themselves. They took a million dollars of cash, which was hidden underneath his closet beneath the floorboards. They knew where all his antiques were hidden. They knew *which ones were most valuable*. Because as you know, he collected a lot of stuff that was worthless, because he just loved it. That's the kind of guy he was. But accidentally, or just as a result of his hoarding, he ended up with some stuff that was incredibly valuable."

"Yeah, I know. He used to show it to me. I would be over there working on the house and I was thinking, you know, that some of that old Tahitian stuff was…"

"Oh yeah, some of those things were taken from villages that had never seen a white man before. They would give him this stuff. And for him it had the sentimental value, you know, but some of these artifacts were hundreds of years old, a thousand years in some cases. One time he had some archeology students from UC Santa Barbara come to see his stuff, and they did the carbon testing. And some of it turned out to be really old, really valuable."

"So someone really knew…"

"Yeah, it's a shame. It's really bizarre, man. I can't explain it."

Pretty soon the bar started filling up, and the sun started melting into the ocean, and I wanted to stay there forever. Life was beautiful here; life was slow. The sunset was sweet. The ocean rolled in, and it rolled out. The rhythm of life was steady and regular. It wasn't all jagged and scary and full of anxiety. People *lived their lives*. They listened to each other. They listened to themselves.

I decided to stay with the mai tai and to really understand it before I moved on to any other drinks. Some regulars showed up, and there were some guys from a wedding at one of the big old hotels on the beach, and the atmosphere was perfect. By the time I left I had talked to everyone in the bar, and everything was so unforced and so natural. I had wanted this. I had craved this.

At some point in the night I noticed a photo behind the bartender sitting next to some bottles of rum. It was a photo of an old man on a yacht in a Hawaiian shirt holding up a giant fish. He had a sly grin on his face. There was something about the face, the grin, the fish, the yacht…there was a story here. I was intrigued. I asked one of the locals next to me who the man in the picture was.

"God rest his soul," said the woman. "That was Sam Bernard."

"Patron saint of Pirate's Cove," said a guy who was with her. "He was the soul of this place."

"He came here all the time," she said. "He even came up with some of the drink recipes. Huge fan of tiki culture."

"Did he die recently?"

"Yeah, he was murdered. Someone broke into his home and shot him. Sad."

That night is fuzzy in my memory, but I do remember a guy who wandered into the bar and ordered a Zombie 151. He was chubby and had spotty facial hair. He was carrying a suitcase and he seemed nervous and distracted. He asked the bartender what time it was several times and the bartender asked him if he needed to be somewhere. The guy replied that he was catching the train to San Francisco at 9:30. He drank his cocktail quickly and he kept looking out the door. He kept rifling through his luggage and looking for things, putting things on the bar. At one point he went to the bathroom. I got up to pretend to look out at the beach. I snuck a peak down at his belongings. He had left a badge on the table that said he worked for "Higgins" something in the IT department. His first name was Devin but the last name was long and I lost my nerve and looked away. In his bag was a passport. I went back to my seat just as he came out of the bathroom.

He finished his drink, ordered a shot of tequila, asked the time, and left at 9:10 or so.

At some point I ambled along on the beach, buzzing with the glow of that place, the waves crashing on the shore in the dark. There's something mesmerizing about the beach at night. I remember sitting for some time on the sand, looking out at the sea, seeing the glowing lights of cruise ships going down to Catalina and Mazatlan. Then I remembered the odd IT guy and my curiosity got the better of me. I walked the several blocks to the old 1920's train station and looked at the schedule. The last train to San Francisco left at 6:00. The 9:30 train was headed to Oceanside, San Diego, and Tijuana. I walked home, puzzled.

Later that night I woke up on the boat, and I couldn't stop thinking about this old man and how strange it was that someone knew exactly how to break into the house and where to find his valuables. They took all that cash! How did they know? Something burned inside me, and wasn't the rum I'm telling you. Something *burned*, my friends! I get like this sometimes – when something doesn't make sense I will not stop until I figure it out. Who would do this? Who *could* do this? It would have to be someone who knew him, right? But who would risk that in such a small town where everyone knows everything about you? It would be so obvious.

This man was the patron saint of this wonderful bar. He was the guiding spirit, the protector and benefactor of this beautiful refuge. To rob and murder someone like this was an abomination. I imagined that the spirit of Sam Bernard was trying to talk to me, to ask me as a new patron of Pirate's Cove to repay him by trying at the very least to figure out who had done this wretched thing.

It was in the middle of these thoughts that I drifted into a rum-soaked sleep on my little houseboat.

2

One night I went for a walk on the beach up north of Pirate's Cove. A weird summer fog had come off the ocean to drift into town and everything was dreamlike as I walked along the beachfront. There were several large, high-end hotels near the marina. I passed those, then I passed a large two-story rental cottage, probably from the twenties. A group of thirty-somethings had rented the place out and they were barbecuing, and the smell of burgers mingled strangely with the cold misty ocean smell. There was a short picket fence separating the yard from the beach. I walked past the house and looked in. Three women were sitting in their bikinis in a hot tub, holding glasses of white wine. Several guys were standing around the barbecue with cans of beer. When the wind blew my way and the ocean waves died down I heard that they were all speaking German.

I passed an empty house with a SOLD sign out front, its brooding exterior glaring angrily at me.

Then I passed an enormous A-frame beach house with a glass wall facing the ocean and saw a movie playing on a huge TV screen. It was something in black and white with Clark Gable. A middle-aged man with a beer gut paced in front of the TV. He wore nothing but a speedo. He turned suddenly and looked at me and I walked on.

Down by the water there were several dark hulking shapes. When the wind came my way I smelled marijuana and it was a strong, funky variety. I saw another old beach cottage with a SOLD sign out in front. Then I passed one of the big old hotels where they were having a wedding reception. The guests had wandered down to the beach with their champagne flutes and gin and tonics, and some of the women were wading in the water holding their dresses up. Some of the men had taken off their shoes and were doing the same. Someone up at the hotel was singing karaoke badly. It was an eighties song that I couldn't identify.

Then a vacant lot with a realtor's name and a big SOLD sign hanging on the fence.

And then I passed an old hotel where the dining room came up to the sand and I looked in on a world of privileged diners eating filet mignon and swordfish and fresh caught lobster. It reminded me of some of the vacations we'd taken when I was a kid. There were kids in there squirming in their seats, playing with their iPhones, their parents reprimanding them and telling them to eat their food.

And then I came to a four-story house, an immense fortress of a place separated from the surrounding structures by tall fences. The gates were closed and the fences were too tall to see over. The second floor had wall to wall glass facing the ocean, and the third floor had a porch. There appeared to be a party in progress on the roof, with snatches of music drifting toward me in the breeze. A man was pacing on the porch high above me, talking angrily into a phone. He held a beer in one hand. He walked unevenly, as if he were on a boat. The waves were deafening at this part of the beach. The lights from the marina looked like glittering orange and white pearls in the misty night. As the man paced violently, I strained to pick out what he was saying. I'm an incurable snoop, by the way. Back in college I used to go through my roommates' closets when they were out of town. I used to go through my mom's room when she was out for the night, looking for anything weird, anything I wasn't supposed to see.

I must've stayed there for twenty minutes in rapt attention. In between waves I only heard a few words. He kept saying "….*told* you to do (CRASH)…not what I fucking told (CRASH)…instructions (CRASH)…listen when somebody fucking gives you…"

After awhile he went back inside, slamming the door. I looked up at the house but couldn't see him. The party was still going on on the roof, invisible to me.

Then he stormed out onto the patio again, on the phone. He was listening this time.

"I will. I WILL."

Waves crashed.

"I have it."

He was silent, listening.

"I will have that, I will have everything for you."

Waves crashed.

"I know. I know."

He hung up and slammed his hands on the railing.

"FUCK!"

Then he went back inside. I walked back to the marina, past all the other oddities. As I walked, two naked girls ran laughing out of a beach house towards the water and, screaming with shock, jumped into the cold Pacific. Must be a dare, I thought, wishing I could be at that party. The beach was a strange mix of locals, snow birds, and Euro-tourists who came for the weekend. There were all the weddings, plus the botanical gardens, the old mission, the wine country. There was a lot to do and the town had made a nice little industry for itself. But how long could a nice town like this avoid over-development? I remembered a little beach town in Mexico, Puerto Piñasco, that my parents had taken me to when I was a kid. When we were there it was a sleepy town with traveling Mariachis that walked up and down the malecon playing for the few tourists who came down from Arizona. I remembered it as an idyllic place, but when I went back later with some college friends it had turned into something resembling Mazatlan. The malecon was full of spring break bars, the marina was full of American yachts, and nothing looked the same. And my college friends all called it Rocky Point.

How much development was too much? I had seen at least one person in Santiago with a shirt that said "Keep Playa Santiago Weird." I wondered why this town hadn't gotten the Puerto Piñasco treatment. Despite all the tourists, it was still so incredibly slow and sleepy. It was very much a town run by and for the locals, and they appeared to want to keep it that way. That's what brought me here.

The next day I went to the Cove as they were opening. The bartender, whose name I had learned was Dave, was filling up the ice bins. "Hey," he said. "What'll it be?"

"No rush. You can get set up, I'm not in a hurry."

"It's no problem. You want a mai tai?"

"Sure."

He made it, gave it to me, and then told me he was going out in the back to get supplies.

"If anyone shows up, you can get them a beer or something."

"Oh, sure," I said. Sure enough, as soon as he went out back a bachelorette party showed up. I was standing near the bar, looking at some of the old photos on the wall, and they must've thought I was the bartender.

"Uh, are you guys open?" said a loud blonde one. "We need to get this girl drunk, like right now."

"Oh, you want some Tecates or something?" I said, walking behind the bar.

"I said DRUNK, dude."

I thought. "Oh, have you tried the fizzy jizz?"

"Yeah!" They screamed amid laughter. "She needs to swallow some fizzy jizz before she gets married!"

"Will it get us loaded?"

"I guarantee."

"Then we'll take eight."

Oh god, what was I doing. What if Dave came back and saw me making shitty drinks at his bar? This was the ultimate trespass.

I looked around quickly. Some cheap vodka was tucked in the back of the vodka case, a strong one they probably kept just for this purpose. Don't waste good vodka on these people. I grabbed it and emptied half of it into a shaker, then filled it with ice. Okay, fizzy jizz. *Jizz*. Coconut milk! I looked around and found some, then poured it into the shaker and shook the damn thing as they laughed and teased the bride, taking selfies, taking pictures of me. Half of them were on their phones. I lined up eight shot glasses on the bar and started pouring the shots, when I remembered this was a *fizzy* jizz. After the glasses were full I winced and gave each one a spritz of soda water. They screamed in delight and passed the drinks around, then made me take a picture of all of them doing the shot together.

"I'm paying," said one of them. "Because Jen paid at the hotel. And remember guys, Courtney does not pay this whole weekend. Do not let her. How much is it?"

"Uh," I thought. Seven bucks each? Sure. "Fifty-six."

She threw eighty bucks at me.

"We need more of those," said the bride, flushing with the cheap booze. I took a deep breath, hoped Dave wouldn't return, and did the whole disgusting routine again. This went against everything this bar stood for, but I guess they had rent to pay. The girls did all the shots, and I got the same eighty bucks again from a different girl, and they went on their way as Dave returned with a box of pineapples.

"Sorry about that," he huffed as he set the box down on the bar. "Who were they?"

"Some bachelorette party. I hope you don't mind, I gave them shots of vodka. I used the cheap stuff."

He laughed and looked at all the cash on the bar. "You're a man after my own heart. I say get them smashed and get them out the door."

I sat down, relieved.

"Were they just vodka shots?"

"I called it fizzy jizz."

"Oh god, what was in it?"

"Vodka, coconut, soda. Hope you don't mind."

"So now everyone's gonna come in here asking for a goddamned fizzy jizz," he said with a smile.

I finished the drink and he started making the next one. "This is on me, for your help," he said, shaking the drink.

Okay, it might not seem very impressive, but remember, this was a big moment for me. Getting the trust of this kind of bartender at this kind of bar doesn't just *happen*. It's something you work at, and when you're in, you're in. It's a matter of trust and attitude. But I don't want to seem too proud. I didn't cure cancer like my parents would've wanted, but this was something.

Dave asked me my name and what I was doing in Santiago. I grumbled out my name and told him the bare details. My dad had died and left me quite a bit of money and here I was, living in my houseboat.

"He must've left you a lot. How did he get that kind of money?"

"Lawyer to the stars."

"Wow."

"Yeah. Celebrity divorces, athletes accused of rape, contract disputes."

He finished shaking the drink and poured it into an old fashioned glass filled with crushed ice. He seemed interested, so I continued as he garnished the drink.

"After my parents divorced I only saw my dad on TV. It turns out he had a lot more money than I realized."

"What did you come here for? Any plans?"

"I've been wanting to come to this place for years, but it was only when my dad died that I was able to."

"How so?"

"He pressured me into going to law school, I hated it, and when he died I bought a houseboat and came here to learn how you make your drinks."

He stared at me. "Are you serious?"

"Those are my plans for the future." I took a sip of the mai tai. "That's all I have on the agenda."

He laughed out loud.

"I've never heard that story. And people come here for a lot of reasons. But never anything like that. And I hope you're patient, because I don't give out the recipes."

"Oh, I'm very patient. But you know what I'm really curious about?" I said. "That old man who was robbed. That's the weirdest story I've heard in a long time. I can't get it out of my mind."

"Oh, forget it. It could've been anyone. They'll never solve it."

"What do you mean?"

"Well, I'll put it like this. I loved the guy. He was the best friend this bar could ever have. This place is on his land, by the way. It was a fishing hut when his great grandfather bought the land in the 1800's and had a ranch here."

"So he was nice to you? Who hated him?"

"First of all, he was my closest friend, okay? A gentleman. But I'm glad I wasn't in business with him, 'cause he didn't get rich by being nice. He made a fortune in real estate, Higgins Properties. You've seen those houses he builds, all over California."

"*Those* things? All those tract homes?"

"Yeah. He was a bit of a cheapskate. He made his share of enemies. You can't really get that rich without pissing off a few people. He had a certain reputation around here. People thought he was pretty cutthroat."

"I think Hilda did it," said a beach bum who had just joined us. He was about forty, his hair was dripping from the ocean, and his surf board was leaning against the wall with the wet suit hanging from a hat rack.

"Who's Hilda?" I asked.

"His ex-wife. She would've fuckin' done it, if I know her, which I do. She was a real…"

"No one in town liked her," Dave said, and started making a drink for the beach bum, who hadn't ordered one.

"You know," said the beach bum, "Sam wasn't really the ruthless business man that people think he was. His business didn't really take off until fifteen years ago. It was really John Bernard that I give the credit to. And a lot of those stories are not totally credible. I mean, a lot of the people who hated him, that was just sour grapes in my opinion."

Dave handed the drink to the beach bum, who apparently was such a regular that no ordering was necessary.

The bar started to fill up, and pretty soon I was in a beautiful tiki haze. The record player was on, and the little pile of old exotica records next to it was the only source of music. Customers would flip the records and choose the next ones. It appeared to be only two or three customers who were bold enough to play DJ. Now it was Ethel Azama's *Exotica*, then it was Esquivel's *Latin-Esque*, then it was Martin Denny's *Quiet Village*. The music was full of flutes and pianos and bongo drums and Theremins playing faux-Arabic and oriental folk songs, Polynesian war dances, Chinese wedding songs filtered through mid-century suburban America and played by white men in the fifties and sixties. The sounds, the taste of the drinks, the waterfalls everywhere, the aquariums filled with spiny, odd-looking, neon fish with huge round mouths and cartoonish beady eyes…all this, plus the local mystery was wonderful. At one point in the night, the bar was full of locals and a couple tourists, and I had been in three conversations with three different groups, and I realized that this bar was a magical place. Every time I looked out at the beach I felt a shiver on my arms and the back of my neck. Warm drafts of air would come in off the ocean and I would thank my dad for giving me this, wondering if I had earned it by suffering his neglect over all these years.

I had decided to only ask a few questions per night about the murder. I wanted these people to like me, not see me as an annoying snoop, which is one of my anxieties. It used to annoy the hell out of my dad when I was growing up, and nothing was worse than his anger, so I had learned to curb it. But that didn't mean I couldn't listen. Carefully. While staring into my drink. And the only notable thing that night was a snatch of something from the bar: "The guy owns the house next door to me, and he's never there. He doesn't even live in town unless he has to come for, you know…." Bar noise rose to a crescendo and died down. "You know where he lives…a huge compound in the Tuscan Estates down there."

"Rancho Santa Fe?"

I looked over. It was two men talking, and the one hearing the information looked off in the distance, shaking his head. It was a look of…what was it? A realization of some great impropriety, of unbelievable misconduct.

And then the bar quieted down and the same guys, a little drunker now, were still talking about the same neighbor. "I'm just saying, it's kind of weird when you're on the city council and you live four hundred miles away."

What was going on here? A city council member who didn't live in Playa Santiago? This had to mean something. I was done with my drink after that, and I paid my tab. I didn't like to leave the bar this way, disturbed, my mind racing, trying to drunkenly put pieces together that didn't add up to anything. But it had happened again. I paced up and down the beach half the night until I wore myself out and passed out on the boat.

I needed more information, damn it.

3

The next time I went to Pirate's Cove there were a couple of regulars who recognized me and we nodded cordially to each other. I ordered the zombie this time, a menagerie of rums, spices, housemade syrups, and fresh grapefruit juice. It was a symphony of sour, sweet, and bitter flavors served with an engraved tiki cup and garnished with a pineapple wedge and umbrella. I said to anyone who would listen, "Does anyone have any theories about Sam Bernard's murder? What about his ex-wife?"

"Hilda Bernard," said a grizzled old fisherman who usually told long rambling fishing stories to anyone who would listen.

"What's the deal with her?" I asked. "Does she live in town?"

"Not anymore. She's in Vegas now. And I hope she stays there."

I nodded and waited. I had to keep myself from asking too many questions. These old guys wanted to talk. All you had to do was plant a seed and wait.

"She wasn't much of a wife," he said, sipping his Tecate.

"Hmm."

"She was in her twenties when they got married. She was something, I'll tell you. No man in this room would've kicked her out of bed for spilling the cottage cheese. I will guarantee you that."

He paused, drank his beer, and continued.

"She was beautiful. But Sam got older, she got restless, she was waiting for him to die, and we all knew it."

He took another long hit off the bottle.

"They got divorced when he found some text messages from another man on her phone. He got some good lawyers, she got nothing, and she was run out of town. And that's the last we saw of her."

"So she would've known the house, known where his antiques were?"

"She knew everything."

I thought.

"And she could've hired some cheap hoodlums to go in there and kill him, make it look like a standard robbery, and take the good stuff so she could finally get the payoff from all those years of marital misery?"

I was getting creative, but it was worth a shot. No one else was trying to solve this thing, so goddamn it someone had to. The bar was silent.

A woman in the corner looked at me. She was a lady named Ivette whom I'd seen in the bar a dozen times and who didn't seem to have a job. A down to earth, salty local probably in her forties.

"Good theory," she rasped in a smoker's voice. "She had the motive. She had the means."

"But you know who else had a motive," said a dapper man I'd only seen once. He was sipping what looked like a Singapore Sling over by the record player, which was playing Arthur Lyman. "Jack McKay."

"He had a motive to kill everyone in town," said Dave, washing glasses with an old white rag behind the bar.

"True, but listen: Jack was outbid by Higgins for all those properties. You know he hated how they bought him out."

"Who's that?" I asked.

"He's a realtor," Dave said. "Sam's company took all his business, they've been buying up homes all over town for years."

"Why?"

"You tell me," said the salty woman in her forties. "You...tell...me."

A misty breeze blew into the bar, and I was frustrated. I looked out to the beach as three girls walked in. One of them was very attractive. I like brunettes, by the way. I don't know why. This one was a brunette, and she was the Platonic ideal. Sweet. Innocent. Curious. Slightly crazy. This all showed in her eyes, in the split second I saw her. Was she a local? She had to be. I could spot tourists by now.

The girls sat in one of the booths and ordered drinks, and I had to fight the urge to look back at them. Finally the interesting one came up to the bar to order drinks, and mercifully she stood next to me.

"Hey, Dave. Can we get two Volcanoes and a Rum sour?"

She looked at me.

"What's that you're drinking?"

"Zombie."

"Get the sour," she said, winking at me. "It's even better."

"I will." I wanted something witty to say, but I was staring at her face, and my wit left me.

She got the drinks and went back to the table. I forgot about my investigation and started thinking about her. Eventually the girls went outside to have a smoke and even though I hate cigarettes I went out there to bum a cigarette. One of her friends obliged me.

"Are you guys locals?" I asked.

"She is," she said, nodding at the attractive one. "We're her friends from college. We're staying at the Churchill."

I nodded. The posh old hotel down by the marina.

We made small talk about the town, the bar, this and that. I told them I was living in the marina, and they were interested. The attractive one was eyeing me. When we finished smoking we all went inside and the next thing I knew her friends were paying their tabs and she was telling them she wanted to stay for one more drink. Her friends gave her that look that girls give each other, when they're concerned. The look says, "Are you sober? Are you sure you want do this? Are you okay?"

The girl waved them off and they left, chattering to each other. She sat next to me at the bar and ordered a rum sour.

"Aren't you going to get one?" she asked.

"I shouldn't."

"You have to try it. It's on me."

We had our drinks and I got up to leave, hoping she would follow.

"I'm on my way out too," she said. "You want to check out the beach?"

"Sure."

It was a warm night and I took off my sandals as we walked on the sand.

"So," I said, "You're a local. What are your thoughts on the murder?"

"Sam Bernard?"

"Yeah."

"It's a pretty fucked up family, you know. Nothing would surprise me. Two ex-wives who hated him. A son with a drug habit and a gambling problem. One son who doesn't even talk to the guy anymore."

"What kind of a guy was Sam?"

"Nice guy every time I met him. He loved this town. He was one of those 'Keep Santiago Weird' people. Really into preservation. Gave tons of money to preserve the mission, that kind of stuff."

"The weird thing is that the people knew exactly where everything was. How to disable the alarm system, where the antiques were."

"Yeah, but he could never keep a secret. He was always telling people everything. If you got the man drunk he would tell you anything you wanted to know. He was always going to antique conventions."

"It makes me think that whoever did it was another antique dealer. They would know which stuff to take and how to sell it, how much it was all worth."

"Yeah, that's what I've thought. But you know, the house was ransacked. All his old books, his office."

"Really?"

We walked in silence for a while.

"Also," she said, "there was another guy who had some issues with him. Have you heard of Sean Topper?"

"No."

"He was a contractor who was sued by Bernard's company for some shoddy work, then he countersued and claimed they hadn't paid him or something. Huge debacle. He hated, hated, hated that company."

"Wait, there was also a son with a drug problem?"

"Yeah, John. He's been sober for ten years though. To be fair. And I don't think he gambles anymore. He has a huge place on the beach. And there's another son who I think lives in Hawaii, but he's not part of the business."

"Wait, I didn't get your name."

"Anna."

I told her my name, and of course we had to talk about it for a few minutes. I wanted to keep seeing her.

"Do you work here in town?"

"Yeah, I work at Playa Roasters. Best coffee on the central coast."

"Is that place up on Central?"

"It is."

"I've seen it. Do you work tomorrow?"

"I do. You should come see me. I do a good pour over."

"I will."

We walked a bit more and I told her I couldn't stop thinking about this murder, and I would be up all night trying to figure it out.

"Want to smoke a joint? Might help you sleep."

"Or I'll come up with some insane conspiracy."

"It might be true, knowing this town."

We smoked the joint and it was a pretty perfect night. For a half hour I forgot about the murder, and I was glad to be alive, and I was with a pretty girl on a beautiful California beach, and all was right with the world. Then she got a text message and looked at her phone.

"My boyfriend wants to know what I'm doing. I'm not going to tell him," she laughed. "Guys generally don't want their girlfriends smoking a joint on a beach at night with another guy."

He was in Portland, in grad school.

"We've known each other for a long time," she said. "He was with me through a lot of bad stuff. We're doing the long distance thing right now." She took a hit of the joint. "It's not easy."

There went my chances. I was little quiet, a little mad that she hadn't told me.

We finished the joint and she said she needed to get home and I said I'd come get some coffee tomorrow, and she walked off into town and disappeared around a corner under the orange street lights.

I walked back up to the huge house I'd seen the other night, with the maniacal man on the cell phone. Was this the son? If so, he'd definitely fallen off the wagon. I stood on the beach trying not to stare obviously at the house. Who knew what kind of security he had there?

I didn't go home because lights were on in the house and at one point one of them was turned off. Someone was home. And then, all of a sudden, the main light in the room facing the ocean was turned on and two men appeared, talking quickly and laughing. They were wearing white button-down shirts, the top few buttons undone. These were the kinds of clothes I'd seen locals wearing when they went out to a bar or a club. The guy I'd seen on the phone was walking around the room, turning on a stereo, taking his wallet and keys and cell phone out of his pockets and throwing them on a table. He went to the fridge and took out a couple of beers, handing one to his friend.

I walked underneath the balcony so I could hear them and wouldn't be seen. The balcony doors opened and I heard them talking above me. The waves were loud again, and I strained to listen.

"How's the house? Everything alright?"

Then waves. Then: "…can't thank you enough…"

Then: "You guys in session…"

"Tomorrow, some committee meetings, public session, then…"

"And things are looking good for us?"

The waves smashed on the beach, and I cursed them. After awhile I didn't hear anything above me. I walked back to the marina, looking back up at the house. The lights were on but I couldn't see anyone. The rental houses showed some signs of life, and so did the hotels of course. But the shuttered houses were even emptier than before, and they glared at me like silent witnesses to murder.

4

The next morning I got up and went to the coffee shop. When I walked in it smelled like fresh croissants and coffee, two of the best smells in the world. These smells tell you that you are in a civilized place. I saw Anna behind the Marzocco pulling espresso shots. She smiled when she saw me and I went to the counter and ordered the Kenya pour over from a skinny guy in his twenties with a sweater and a large mustache. The coffee was five bucks. They obviously took the coffee seriously at this place. I respected that. I watched her slowly pour the hot water into the filter, a little bit at a time. She would poke at the grounds with a swizzle stick, then smell it, then pour some more water. It took about seven minutes to get the coffee, which was strong and smooth without a hint of bitterness. This was the kind of place where a barista would talk to a customer for ten minutes about the party they were both at the night before, and where everyone seemed to know each other and you sometimes couldn't tell customers from employees. Anna came over to me.

"How are you feeling?" she asked. "I probably shouldn't have had that last rum sour last night."

"Yeah, me neither. I'm not at my best."

"So have you seen the town much, or have you confined yourself to Pirate's Cove?"

"I haven't left the sand too often since I got here."

"Well, I get off at twelve if you want a tour."

"Sure. Should I come here?"

"Yeah, I'll drive."

I went to a little Mexican place for a breakfast burrito, then went to the beach and watched the pasty Midwestern tourists swimming with their pasty kids, then I went to pick up the Santiago Sentinel. The news was charmingly boring, small town stuff. I finally went back to the coffee shop and she was finishing up. When she came out she motioned me over to her car and we got in.

"The first part of our tour will be interesting to you," she said, driving through the tree-lined streets up the hill and away from the beach. We arrived at a palatial estate, only partially visible through a line of tall juniper trees. A curving driveway sloped up through a brown, uncut lawn to the house. The whole place was surrounded by a tall, spiked iron security fence.

"This is it," she said.

"Is this the house?" I asked, incredulous.

"The house of murder. You want to go have a look?"

"Is no one living there?"

"Not anymore." She got out and we looked around. The driveway had a gate that had once evidently supplied security, but the gate was open today. The grass hadn't been mowed and the flowers were dying. It looked like it had been a secure house. If the gate had been closed the night Sam Bernard was killed, the killers would have needed the code.

No neighbors were around, and we walked up the driveway to the house and walked around to the side. It was enormous. There were tennis courts in back, and we walked to a side window to look in at his library. The place was in pristine shape. You couldn't believe anyone had been killed in there.

"Let's go in back, I think we can –"

A car raced up the street and turned immediately into the driveway, coming to a screeching stop at the front. We ran behind some bushes and got down on the ground. A car door opened and someone walked to the front door and went in. We looked at each other with wide eyes. The person must've been inside for ten minutes, but it was endless for me, lying on the ground terrified. Finally the door shut and the person got back in the car and sped down the driveway. Instantly Anna was running back to the car and I was following her. We got to the car just in time to see the car ahead of us, far down the hill, turning right. We gave chase, Anna following at a distance and barely picking up the trail. The car, a black Lincoln town car, was heading to the coast.

"Where are they going?" Anna asked. "Are they going up to Duke's Beach?"

"What's that?"

"Just a really remote place that only locals go. It's kind of a druggy place where the kids go to smoke pot. It's an unofficial nude beach at night."

We followed the town car down winding coastal roads, through lightly forested terrain, north of town. The road suddenly opened up onto a stunning view of the ocean, and we were on a cliff high above the beach. The car suddenly turned off on an unmarked dirt road and disappeared in dust. We followed.

"Duke's Beach," she said. "I knew it."

The road curved dramatically in a dizzying descent down the mountain, and then we were driving along the beach on a narrow road, following the Lincoln. The Lincoln pulled over to the side and Anna passed it.

"We're just a couple of locals going to the beach," she muttered, looking in the rear view mirror. "That's all that's happening. We're not following you."

She casually pulled over.

"Let's go to the beach, Aristotle. This is the next stop on our tour."

We walked over to the beach, a pleasant spot secluded in a cove and surrounded by towering cliffs. We walked toward the water and sat on the sand, and Anna looked back casually and gasped.

"That's…oh my God, that's…"

"Who? WHO?"

"Hilda Bernard."

"His ex-wife? What is she doing?"

"She has something. It's a box."

I looked back. She was a very good looking, well-taken-care-of woman in her mid thirties. She wore jeans and a t-shirt, and she did indeed hold a box, and she walked to the ocean without seeing or noticing us. She walked into the water until it was up to her knees, and with a cry, heaved the box into the waves.

She held her face in her hands, shaking, and walked back to the car, which she pounded with her fists, unleashing another cry of grief, rage, whatever it was. She got back in the car and drove back up the winding road to the coast highway.

As soon as she left we were running to the water. The waves had torn the box apart and dispersed the contents, which seemed to be many sheets of paper. Most of them had washed out too far for us to get to, but a few had come to the shore. Anna picked up several.

"Wow," she said. "No wonder he married her."

I looked. They were nude photographs of Hilda. And they were…wow.

I scanned the waves and saw some more sheets, and I waded in and got two of them. They were deposition transcriptions for their divorce proceedings.

"What was she doing? Why did she want to get rid of these?" I asked.

"Maybe there was evidence she wanted to get rid of."

"This stuff doesn't really prove anything. It seems like stuff he had in his closet somewhere."

"But how did she get in the house?" Anna asked. "Did she still have a key after that shitty divorce?"

We sat down on the beach with our papers. They didn't add up to anything. The depo notes were very mundane, just basic questions about the couple's finances. But what else had been thrown away?

"Okay, here's what I think. I think she hired some goons to sneak –"

"Goons?"

"Yeah, she hired the goons to steal his antiques and they fucked up and went there on the wrong day, he wasn't supposed to be there, and they freaked out and killed him. Maybe he tried to fight them or something. She didn't want this to happen, and she was just trying to get rid of anything that would show her motives. Maybe there were notes that showed how broke she would be after the divorce. Maybe there were documents showing how much his antiques were worth, proving she knew that info. Maybe there were documents, emails, letters showing threats she had made. But she said she would kill him. People say that stuff in divorces, when money is involved. Especially if she's as crazy as everyone says she was."

"Oh, she was crazy," Anna said, taking off her shoes and lying back on the sand. "Everyone in town knew how crazy she was. Well, I think you solved it, Aristotle. You sure take after your namesake."

"You know, Aristotle was the greatest philosopher of all time. All of western thought comes from him. Not from Plato. And I don't want to hear you claim otherwise."

"I'll take your word for it. What are you doing in this town, anyway?"

"I don't know," I said. "Not much. I just wanted to drop out for awhile, collect myself. I really came to learn how those drinks are made at Pirate's Cove."

"Oh, good luck," she said. "My dad tried to figure out those recipes for years. He finally gave up."

"What are you doing in Santiago?" I asked.

"I was raised here. I went to college and I was gonna move to New York with my friends but my mom got sick. She didn't have anyone to take care of her, so here I am. She just needs extra help, that's all. She still works, she does real estate."

"Your parents are divorced?"

"Yep. My dad lives in Seattle."

"You know," I said, "I need to get this murder out of my mind. Since I solved it, I need some space. I need to get away from that bar for awhile."

"Have you been to wine country?"

"I have not."

"It's pretty nice. Free wine samples."

"Let's go."

"Okay, but I need just a few more minutes of sun."

"Sure."

When she was ready we drove back down the coast and headed out of town, through some winding hilly terrain, until we came to a valley to the southeast of the city. It was a long valley and we drove past a few cattle ranches and orchards until we came to the vineyards. We stopped at the Roberts Ranch, one of the less touristy of the lot. The vineyard was on both sides of the road, stretching into the foothills. We stopped in front of an old farmhouse and walked into the tasting room. A few locals were in there. It was the middle of the week so that's probably why the weddings and bachelorette parties hadn't invaded. We sat at the bar and a middle aged woman gave us a menu. They had a pinot, a cab, a rosé and sauvignon blanc. She put a plate of nuts in front of me and I started eating.

"So, you know, the etiquette is really to buy something," Anna told me. "Either a glass or a bottle. I mean, they'll give you samples, but you really should buy something."

I got a sample of the cab. She got the pinot. Mine was good.

"Hmmm," I said. "I'm getting blackberry. A little oaky. Some mineral content, very nice. Very balanced."

"Notes of grape."

"That's in there, for sure."

"Alright, Daddy Warbucks," Anna said after we'd had a few samples. "You're the one with the houseboat. I say you buy us a couple bottles and we go drink 'em on the beach."

"What sounds good? A white and a red?"

"You choose."

I got a pinot grigio and a cabernet, which set me back about thirty bucks a piece. We walked out into the afternoon sun as a car pulled up and three men got out. Two of them were the ones I'd seen at the beach house the other night, and the third one, who carried a couple of rolled up blueprints in his arms, I didn't recognize.

"Anna," said the one with the blueprints.

"Hi, Sean. How are you?"

"Great, how's your dad?"

"He's good."

"Say hi to him for me."

As we left, the party went over to a picnic table outside the farmhouse and spread the blueprints out to look at. One of the men, the owner of the house, went inside and came out with some bottles of wine. Anna and I sat in the car watching this.

"Okay, we should go," she said. "They're gonna notice."

"Who are those guys?"

"That's John Bernard, Sam's son. That is Glenn Evans, he's on the city council. And the guy I know is a contractor."

"Didn't you say John Bernard had a drug problem?"

I watched him take a big old sip out of his wine glass.

"Yes. He can't even be near booze. This is very weird."

We got back in the car and drove back to town. We parked at her mom's place, a couple blocks from the beach, where she lived in an old Airstream in the back yard. She let me peek in and I saw that she had the place decorated in some pretty great vintage midcentury furniture. We walked down to the beach with our bottles. Luckily I had a bottle opener on my boat, and we spent the afternoon drinking some excellent local wine. My brain was fried and we didn't try to solve mysteries that whole afternoon. At one of the hotels someone had hired a Mariachi band for a party, and we heard them in the distance and the sound mingled with the waves. It was a warm afternoon. The sun went down and she said she should be getting home, and I thanked her for the tour and I went back to the boat.

Later that night I saw the Mariachi band taking their break on the beach with their instruments lying in the sand. They were playing guitar and laughing.

I didn't go back to Pirate's Cove for a few days. I needed to let things percolate, get away from the murder. When I did, it was earlier in the day so I wouldn't see people and be drawn back into the mystery. There was too much weirdness and it didn't add up. But for some reason as I was drinking my first Pooka Pooka Bowl people started showing up in pairs and threes. A few were locals and a few weren't. Then I noticed a middle-aged woman on her own, sitting down at the end of the bar. She was chubby and red-faced and unfamiliar to me. Dave was talking to her like a local. From their conversation I gathered that he'd known her parents and that she worked with the Coastal Commission. During a break in the conversation I asked her if she lived in town.

"I grew up here. I live in Sacramento, but I come down a few times a year to see old friends."

"So you must've heard about the murder. Sam Bernard."

"I did. That was too bad."

"Seems to be a lot going on with that family. A lot of drama. I can't help but wonder if…"

"If what?"

"Well, I've been thinking about it, and I've been asking around a lot. And a lot of scenarios come to mind. Considering some of the family drama."

Her face got very tense and she looked down at her drink.

"What happened to that family was a random tragedy. It could've happened to anyone. And it's not very responsible to make crazy accusations."

"No, I'm not, I'm just…I'm just wondering. The whole thing is pretty suspicious, that's all. I mean, whoever did it knew exactly…"

"You're not from here, are you?" she said. "You're a tourist, right? Well, these are local issues. I knew that family. I've known them for over forty years. I loved that old man like a father. He babysat me, he went golfing with my dad. He was a crazy old man, but we loved him. He was stuck in his ways, and he was unwilling to change with the times. But we tried to work with him. I mean, they really…just…"

She struggled to finish her thoughts.

"People should mind their own business. That's the biggest problem with this town. That's why I don't live here anymore."

She stopped. I would've let her continue, but that was all she was willing to say. Someone rescued her, a man I'd seen a few times at the bar. He came over and saw that her drink was low and bought her another one. He gave me an irritated look. I looked at Dave to see if he knew what was going on here. He saw my gaze and turned away.

Things were awkward, so I took my Pooka Pooka Bowl out on the patio and looked at the waves crashing, crashing endlessly. The bar was too crowded and the energy was not good. Something had happened. I paid my tab and went home. This woman was clearly friends of the family and had a strong incentive to perpetuate the idea that it was a random break-in. What was that about the old man not changing with the times? And why be so defensive about the idea that the thieves knew too much about the house for it to be random? The lady did protest too much. But I couldn't quite figure out why.

5

Anna was going to a party at a friend's house and she was pretty sure that I was free that night, so she invited me. It was a friend of hers from high school who had also moved back after college and now rented a big house up the hill with some other friends.

I met Anna at her house at around eight and we walked about half a mile up the hill, sharing a joint I'd watched her role in the Airstream. The house was on a hillside overlooking the town, and it was an old run-down place fit for a group of people in their twenties. There were about fifteen people there, some in the kitchen, some in the living room watching a game, and some in the backyard gathered around the fire pit. There was an upstairs area where no one was hanging out.

I looked at the alcohol, and it was Popov vodka and sprite, and some cranberry juice. Jesus Christ. How could people live like this, drinking corn syrup and rotgut booze? For a few extra bucks and little extra work they could easily get something better. I hunted around and finally found a bottle of wine from one of the local vineyards. At least someone had some taste at this party. I wanted to meet the person and shake their hand.

Anna introduced me to Kelsey, who lived there. "Kelsey works at her mom's catering company here in town." We had some small talk. The company worked with weddings and corporate events at the wineries and other popular tourist venues. The food was really good, super local and organic, and business was good. There was a guy named Bumble who lived next door. He was about fifty and had a large goatee and one missing tooth that showed when he grinned, which was often. I talked to Bumble for awhile after looking around and seeing all the hipsters and realizing that he was probably the most interesting one there. He'd been a professional lumberjack and hunter but now led Sasquatch hunting tours on the north coast and in the Sierras. You paid him to take you to the main migratory routes and breeding grounds, and you camped out for a couple of days with this guy. He had seen over fifty Sasquatches in his life and could recognize certain individuals year after year when passing through on their way up and down the Pacific Northwest.

There was another guy studying to get his associate's degree at Santiago City College and hopefully transfer to Santa Barbara to major in archaeology. He'd been a longshoreman down in San Pedro for a couple of years after high school but came back up here during a strike. He chain smoked and drank a Negro Modelo while he talked to me, out by the fire.

There was a girl who made bracelets and necklaces and sold them online. There were a lot of attractive girls as a matter of fact. As the party grew, there were a few more middle aged folks which was a welcome addition. At one point I ended up talking to a clean cut young guy about Star Wars for twenty minutes before I asked him what he did and he said he was a cop here in town.

Yes, reader, I asked him about the murder. But you'd be proud of me: I meandered into the subject. I almost let him bring it up. I asked him about being a cop in a small town, joked that it sounded like a show on the Lifetime network, then realized that sounded insulting, and then changed the subject by asking about the Sam Bernard case.

"Yeah, I almost got into trouble on that," he said, shaking his head.

"What happened?"

"I was called to the scene, you know, and I'm a rookie cop, and I'm still learning what you do and don't do. Well, I just went out of line, I guess."

"How so? I have no idea how the police force works." I tried to sound fascinated by the inner world of cops.

"Well, the detective is in charge. Always. He calls the shots, he tells you what to do. And my dumb ass didn't realize that. But the thing is…"

He stopped and drank his beer.

"He was ignoring some things. Basic evidence."

"That's weird."

"He just went in and started telling us how the thieves broke in, where and when they shot him, how they looked around to find valuables, and freaked out when they heard the neighbors, and then left in a panic. The whole thing took ten minutes. Like these people just stumbled into this house and it could've been any house, and they had no idea who he was. But what got me into trouble is I said to him, 'Don't you realize that they were here for many hours after they shot him?' Because they had gone through the entire library, book by book. They were looking for something. And all the books they put back on the shelf. This was in addition to drilling a hole in the floor to get to the cash he'd stored in there."

"How did you know this about the books?"

"The maid wasn't there when it happened, but she told us that the books were all in the wrong places, and we found a couple of pages that had fallen out while they were looking through them. I mean, we're talking about hundreds and hundreds of books. And she dusts them every week, so she knew that they had *all* been taken down and put back. So these guys were in the house for a long, long time after they killed the guy."

"Strange."

"I mean, these guys were professionals. They were like people in the movies who are brought in from Europe to steal the crown jewels from some museum. The best in their field. My guess is they'll never find who did this. They left no fingerprints at all. No clues. No one saw any cars on the street that night. And there was a neighbor who walked his dog at nine, and spent the next two hours on the porch smoking cigars. He was staring at the street that whole time. And another neighbor who couldn't sleep and was out in his yard drinking beer from like twelve to two AM. No one saw or heard *anything*."

He took a sip of the Negro Modelo.

"Anyway, I mentioned some of this stuff, which was really stupid. And the detective got really mad at me and threatened me with disciplinary actions and I was taken off the case. I was writing speeding tickets on the coast highway for the next two weeks."

He was swept up in another conversation and then someone was passing around shots of shitty vodka, which I politely declined. After the shots someone shouted something about swimming in the reservoir, and people started heading outside the house. Anna found me and asked if I wanted to go, it was just up the hill. I said sure. We all walked up to the large, dark reservoir, which was behind a fence. We all crawled through a hole in the fence and pretty soon everyone was taking off their clothes and jumping in.

"Aren't you gonna swim?" Anna asked me.

"It looks cold."

"I dare you."

"If you go I'll go."

She took off her shirt and started undoing her bra and I saw that she was serious. So pretty soon we were both in the cold water, our bare skin shivering in the night air, swimming in the dark with everyone else. The sky was a lovely black-purple canopy flecked with stars. The sounds of laughing and shouting echoed against the hillside.

After the swim I was shivering and putting my pants back on when I looked down the canyon and saw what I thought was the old man's house.

"Hey," I said to Anna, "is that Sam Bernard's place?"

She looked down the canyon, shivering and pulling her pants on over wet underwear.

"It is."

The darkened house seemed very, very empty. I didn't know why I couldn't let this murder go. He was an eccentric man with a complicated legacy, who maybe had a lot of good intentions and was killed before he had a chance to set things right. To be taken before you can say goodbye, or apologize, or fix your mistakes, was the saddest of all fates.

As we gazed, a light flicked on in the house. We looked at each other.

"What is that?" I said. "No one should be in there, right?"

"Not at all."

"What's going on?"

"Let's go see," she said.

We walked down with everyone else, and turned off on a side street, then walked through a grassy alley and down another street, and pretty soon I was lost. Then we turned onto Bernard's street and walked up to the looming mansion on the hill. We walked in through the gate and stood in the driveway, looking at the main windows, which were lit up from inside. Then a click from behind us made us whirl around. There was nothing, just a couple of cars parked on the street like normal. And then I saw movement inside one of them, a black sedan with black windows.

"Someone's in the car," I murmured, and started walking out onto the street. She followed and we walked quickly, and there was no sound behind us. As we approached the side street I heard the movement of wheels on gravel, and I turned and saw the car moving slowly down the street towards us. It had started silently, like an electric car. We started running, and the car sped up. She led me to the alley, and we ran in and hid in some tall bushes as the car stopped in front of the alley. I poked my head out and saw nothing behind the black windows. The car idled there silently for about twenty awful seconds before it rolled on down the street. I ran out to look at the license. What I saw confused me: police lights on the rear window. This was an undercover police car.

6

The next day at Pirate's Cove I ordered a Mexican Mai Tai, made with Tequila and a splash of Mexican Coke, and sat there enjoying the new take on the old classic. Dave said a Mexican fisherman had created the drink in the 90's. He'd been a regular while he was living in town and kept asking for a mai tai with these strange specifications. He was apparently trying to recreate something they used to drink in his village in Mexico, but it was never quite right. He ordered it every day, though, and eventually other customers started ordering it. The guy moved away after awhile and was never heard from again. He didn't speak much English, but he used to sit at the bar with a faraway smile on his face, looking at the sea. This was all according to Dave, so you can take it with a grain of salt if you want.

Someone brought a guitar that night, and the regulars all sat around singing old 70's songs, some Bacharach, some Jim Croce, a few Bread tunes, some Steely Dan. I'd been talking about Sam Bernard with Dave, telling him about my adventure the other night at the house, and I went out to the beach to take a leak in the darkness. As I was walking back to my drink I saw a guy from the bar smoking on the patio. He eyed me. He was heavyset, with a couple days of stubble. He didn't look healthy but there was a spark in his eyes.

"Funny to hear you talking about the Bernard case," he said. "I've been working on that for some time."

I stopped.

"Do you work with the police?"

"No," he said. "The Santiago Times."

"Have you learned much?"

"Everything I learn brings me back to one person," he said, and took a drag, looking off at the waves. I waited.

"Hilda Bernard," he said, almost mouthing the words.

"Really? Why?"

"She had the motives, and there were documents of her threatening to kill the guy. She knew everything: how to get in there, how to steal the stuff, how to make it look like a robbery. She knew people who could do it too."

"Really?"

He nodded. "She had criminal connections from her time in Vegas, when she was stripping."

I took all this in.

"The problem is," he said, taking a drag and exhaling it through his nose, "no one talks to me in this town. That's the shitty thing about being a small town reporter."

"How come they haven't arrested her?"

"She got rid of all the evidence that could bring her to trial," he said. "All those documents, everything. And the police don't want to investigate it for some reason. It makes me think something bigger is going on. She's related to a congressman for this district, you know."

"Really?"

"Yeah. Dan Beckman, state senator for District 24. I'm just saying. But the more I ask, the less people want to talk."

He paused. "I've noticed people talk to you around here." He fished around in his pocket and took out a card. "Let me give you this. If you can get any more information, shoot me a message. Anything you tell me will be totally confidential of course."

I looked at the card. Joseph Duquesne.

"That's Du-cain," he pronounced. I nodded. "There's something about you. You have an innocent face. People trust you."

He smoked again.

"See the guy in there with a big ponytail? Def Leppard shirt?"

I looked in the crowded room. They were singing the Marshall Tucker song "Can't You See." There was a guy swaying his head, singing loudly with his eyes closed. He knew every word to the song. He matched the description.

"Yeah, I see him."

"He comes here often. And when he's not here, he's at the bar in the California Inn. And when he's not there, he cleans boats at the Marina."

"Okay. I might've seen him down there, actually."

"When Hilda got divorced from Sam Bernard, that's the guy she was seeing. He's the one who broke up the marriage. He won't talk to me. I'd kill to get his story."

"Okay, I'll try to talk to him if I get the chance."

"Don't mention my name. Don't say anything about me. Now go inside before he sees us talking. I'll be in in a few minutes."

"Okay, well, nice talking to you." I offered my hand.

"Can't shake. Just go inside."

"Wait – what's the guy's name?"

"Eugene English."

I went back inside but I couldn't enjoy my drink and the bar got too noisy and I needed to think. I paid my tab and paced on the beach for awhile before going home. Another local trying to pin it on Hilda Bernard. But when I saw her at the beach she seemed more like a distraught ex-wife throwing away relics from a ruined marriage. That was just my intuition, but who knew? My intuition hasn't always been spot on. In fact, it's gotten me into…never mind. I'll spare you the details. That's for another book; if I get started I'll go on a tangent.

The next day I was at the California Inn, wandering through the lobby looking for the bar. I hoped my sandals and shorts were okay for a ritzy establishment like this, but I was relieved when I got to the bar and saw hotel people who'd just walked in off the beach to get a beer and bowl of fries. It was a fancy place, no doubt – built in the twenties by the looks of it. But the attraction at this bar was the view of the ocean, and probably not the drinks or the food. From the street this was the first floor, but on the beach side it was the second floor, and it felt like you were hovering over the ocean waves. The whole bar looked out on the water with wall to wall glass and as you had your drink you could imagine that you were at the bow of a ship sailing to Tahiti. The bar was not too packed and there was just one bartender, a younger guy. My heart sank. The young ones were never serious about mixing drinks. They were always students or musicians in a shitty rock band and this was usually a day job for them. I sat down and braced myself for a disappointing experience. Eugene English didn't seem to be here.

As I always do when I don't know what kind of place I'm at, I ordered a beer until I could watch him make a few drinks. Then I would decide. They had something local on tap called Bad Dawg Ale, so I got one and it was cold and crisp. He put some freshly fried chips in front of me, and all was okay with the world for the time being. Soon enough he came by and asked if I was staying here.

"No, just staying in a house boat in the marina. A lot of locals come by?"

"It's really a lot of tourists, really. Except for this guy," he nodded to a guy at the bar with a beer and a newspaper. "This guy comes in to make trouble a couple times a week."

"And he waters down my drinks," said the guy, looking up. "So I started ordering beer."

"I'm just doing what your wife told me to do," the bartender said.

"Hey, hey, hey. Here's the thing to remember about my wife: what Sherry tells you to do, *do the opposite*. ALWAYS."

They both laughed. I couldn't ask for Eugene English. No sane person would do that. Unless he was a hired killer of some kind. Which I wasn't.

"I just like the places where the locals hang out," I said. "I've been at Pirate's Cove a lot lately. It's got a real local vibe."

"We get locals here some times," said the guy at the end of the bar. "When they do the open mic nights here, people show up."

"You're right, you're right," said the bartender. "And Gene comes by a lot."

"He's always here, he should pay rent."

"He doesn't need to, the way he tips."

"Who's that?"

"Gene is…" The bartender faltered. "Jimmy, how would you describe Gene?"

"I'm just trying to get a sense of the locals around here," I said.

"Gene English?" said Jimmy. "God. You know, you just have to meet him. He'll probably show up tonight. If you're trying to get a sense of the locals, he's the place to start."

"Gene," said the bartender, making a valiant attempt, "is one of the smartest guys I've ever met. Is that fair, Jimmy? Would you say that?"

Pause. "Yeah. Yeah. He's also one of the weirdest."

"He's very spiritual. Very spiritual. Not in the conventional sense though. And he knows about everything. I mean, he can talk to you for hours about the moon landing, or Calvin Coolidge, or he'll just recite Wordsworth to you if he's in the mood."

"He's also one hell of a musician," said Jimmy. "He can play beautiful guitar."

"Did you know he spent three months at a meditation retreat in Patagonia?" the bartender asked Jimmy. "The southernmost point of the continent. He lived in a tent on a windy plateau down there and just meditated for three months. He lived on rice and yerba mate."

"Did he go to college, or what?" I asked. "How'd he get so smart?"

"I don't know, I think he just reads a lot, he's traveled a lot. That sort of thing."

"No, he went to Harvard for a year," Jimmy said. "He told me that. He dropped out after a year. He was studying engineering."

At this point someone ordered a Long Island Iced Tea and the bartender, whose name according to his nametag was Gabriel, proceeded to make said drink. I watched in fascination as he dutifully measured some bottom shelf vodka, gin, rum, and tequila, threw them all in a Collins glass, sprayed some cola out of the tube, poured a jigger of DeKuyper sweet and sour, and absent-mindedly dropped a few ice cubes and a straw into the glass. He put the disaster on a napkin and said, "That'll be fifteen. Keep it open?"

The whole thing was done with the *joie de vivre* of a coroner's assistant. The liquor was shit, the kind of stuff that was distilled in San Jose or Dallas. The rest was corn syrup, and it was a mockery. I couldn't hang around here all night waiting for this guy to show up. I also couldn't believe this was the guy who broke up this marriage.

I left and wondered if I could go back there and support this aging corporate monstrosity just to find out more about Eugene English. I wasn't sure.

7

I ended up going back to the California Inn two more times, drinking the same beer and watching the same well-meaning bartender mix sad imitations of various cocktails to unknowing customers, waiting for some sign of this guy that Joseph Duquesne seemed to think was a lynchpin in this increasingly muddled case.

The second time at the bar I decided it wasn't even worth it if anymore. Eugene English, no matter how important he was, was not worth patronizing this bar. Going there was like waiting at a dentist's office. I was at the boat later that week on my deck one afternoon, playing a CD of sea chanteys on my ratty old stereo and surveying the scene at the docks. There were the usual fishermen coming back from their daily battle with Neptune. These were dirty, salty men, faces leathery from endless sun, hands hardened from ropes, scaly fish, fishing line, and salt. They spoke gruffly and loudly to each other. There were the rich guys with their yachts, going out for a spin with the family or a client. There was one old black guy who did burials at sea. For 45 bucks an hour he would take you and your loved one's ashes out to sea, dispose of them in an elegant and loving ceremony, perform necessary religious rites, and give you the GPS coordinates of the location so you could go back later. Return visits were offered at a discount.

I was musing on these new neighbors of mine, and bemoaning my failure to find Eugene English, and wondering where I would go next to find him, when I heard a shuffling of feet behind me accompanied by a grunt. I whirled around and saw Eugene standing there, carrying a giant bucket of cleaning supplies – squeegees, mops, etc. He wore a tattered t-shirt with a picture of Jacob Miller on it, singing passionately with his eyes closed, dreadlocks flying. Eugene's sweaty blonde hair was not in a ponytail and it dangled from his head, surrendering itself to gravity.

"Pretty hot out here," I said, not believing my luck.

He sighed. "I've been working since eight. Cleaning boats."

"Want a beer? I've got cold ones."

"Dude, are you…" He looked at me in disbelief. "That's exactly what I need right now."

"Come on board," I said, but he was already doing that. Before I could invite him to sit he was sitting, leaning back while I went into my fridge and got him one of the local lagers I'd found at the liquor store up the street.

"Oh nice," he said as I gave it to him. "I know these guys. Super nice guys. Great beer too. Have I seen you at…" He searched his memory.

"Pirate's Cove."

"Oh, yes! That's right. How are you, man? How have you been?"

"Great."

"I haven't gotten your name."

"Aristotle McCreadie."

"Dude, you're…no shit. Yeah, Dave was telling me about you. He said you were like this really cool, smart, soulful dude who just showed up one day and lives in a houseboat and you've like become his honorary tiki brother."

I was more honored than I showed.

"Really? That's nice of him."

"Yeah, he said you had a really strong, peaceful energy. Nice to know you, man." He raised his beer and we toasted.

Getting information out of Eugene English was the easiest thing I have ever done. In my life. Ever.

The man just wanted to talk. He was curious about me, he was generous, he was open, he didn't think it was weird that I wanted to know all about him. I won't paraphrase – this is basically what he said, the way he said it (*sans* my questions):

"I live out in Madera Valley, it's like a half hour from here. My family has a cattle operation out there. It's been in our family since, I don't know. Five generations. Since the 1800's. It's strictly grass-fed, pastured cows and we rely completely on well water to irrigate the property. I mean, we put our sweat and tears into this, man, but it's so worth it. These are happy cows, and it's some of the best steak you'll ever eat. I mean, my dad gets to know every cow on the property. We have three ranch hands, and they're basically this one family that's been on the property for like three generations as well. The Ramirez brothers, Pedro and Salvador and Pedro's son Alberto. So it's a small operation and…"

I was so entranced by the voice and the idyllic image he was painting that I kind of forgot why I was interested in him, but I know that at some point I was so obviously enraptured by the farm that he offered to take me out there for some steaks that afternoon. I asked if my friend could come and he said no problem.

"I just have one more boat to clean and then I'm ready to go."

I thanked him, said I'd be ready when he was, and texted Anna to come down here immediately so we could go to Eugene's farm. She replied that she didn't know who the hell Eugene was or why I was going to his farm but she'd be here. And she arrived just as Eugene was done for the day. He came by the boat and we were all ready to go.

It was a long, long summer day. The kind of day that lasts until 8:30, where the sun makes long orange and pink streaks on the clouds, and the shadows get longer and the light gets more orange and the heat of the day finally abates as the night breeze takes over. He drove us in an old VW van through the hills and into the valley with the windows open, and the smells of sage brush, grass and eucalyptus came in with the breeze.

I wanted to live at their farm. Even Anna, who'd spent her whole life in this town, was looking around like she wanted to move in. It was in a valley with a river running next to the road as you drive through it. A few orchards, orange groves, and vineyards were in the valley, but all the hills were public space. Cows wandered on the green pastures all around us. He explained the operation, the incredible length of time it takes to get a cow to market size when it eats just grass, and the different characteristics of a grass-fed cow. One of the farm hands was walking by as we toured the property, and Eugene spoke perfect Spanish to him in a brief exchange.

"Yeah, so Salvador says they have some good cuts that they just butchered yesterday if you guys are hungry."

Yes, I was hungry.

"Great, we can grill out back. Let's just go see what they have."

We walked into a barn and he opened up a large refrigerator, revealing a beautiful display of individually wrapped cuts from every part of the cow. He picked up a piece.

"I would really recommend the t-bone, because the thing is you have the tenderloin here, the smaller part, and the strip, that bigger part on the other side of that bone there. Any time you eat meat of course you want the bone in it, if possible. You're gonna get some good marble-ization here," he indicated with his finger. "Sound good?"

"Of course."

Anna wanted something more manageable, so he offered the filet mignon.

We went out to a big barbecue which he loaded with wood ("This is apple wood from the neighbor down the road") and he proceeded to cover the steaks with salt, pepper and olive oil. He went back into the farmhouse and came back with a big bundle of asparagus ("We grow it on the property"). Soon he had a carafe of wine and we were sitting at a picnic table and I was very, very happy. He asked me about myself, what I was doing here. I told him. I actually forgot for over an hour that I had initially wanted to ask him about Hilda Bernard, and I felt bad because now I was starting to like this guy and he had no idea I was using him to solve a mystery. I told him I'd buy him a drink next time he came to Pirate's Cove and made him promise to tell me next time he was going. We exchanged phone numbers. Anna appeared to be enjoying herself. Pretty soon he threw the meat on the grill, and one of the best smells in the world filled the air: steak grilling over a wood fire.

Eugene's dad wandered by, dirty from gathering brush, and said hi. He was a weathered, kindly, down to earth man who had spent his life in the most beautiful place I'd ever seen. You really could've been in Tuscany. There was a quiet glory on his face, and I envied him.

The steak was amazing. I would try to describe the flavor, but it is outside my powers of description and I defer to the professional food critics.

Eventually, as the day was getting late, I mentioned the Bernard murder. He shook his head.

"I feel weird about that whole thing."

I waited, took a sip of wine.

"His wife…well, his ex-wife, well you've probably heard around town, but the old man was getting so crazy and…well, I knew what we did was wrong. Shit. I don't know, we fell in love."

"He knew about it?"

"He found out. Listen: the guy was out of touch with reality. There's this old nutcase who lives over in French Canyon who convinced Bernard that some of his antiques were cursed, because he'd taken them from a sacred spot in Tahiti. They were these crazy tiki gods, carved in wood. They look like big trolls, you know. You've seen them in cheesy restaurants, but these ones were real. So Bernard started thinking he was cursed because he'd taken these things from their rightful place, and this old guy in French Canyon, he's into the occult and he claims he talks to spirits and he thinks the Spanish left a big stash of stolen gold up here, which he's been trying to find for forty years, and he thinks the native spirits are guarding it. I don't know. Hilda told me all this. She said Bernard was paranoid, he would freak out and threaten her, he thought he'd committed a sin by taking these relics. Hilda said he was full of guilt for all his ruthless business dealings and his stolen artifacts."

"What was this guy's name, the paranormal guy?"

"Oh, man, what was his name…everyone just called him Red. But his real name, let me think…Grover. Grover Simpson. I met him when I was a kid, he was an old red-haired dude with a big beard and pretty soon Bernard wouldn't talk to anyone else, and Grover became like his spiritual advisor."

"Weird."

"Yeah. I've stopped talking to people about it, because the police fuckin' talked to me and they can't pin shit on me. I told them what was going on between Hilda and me, and I had nothing to do with that shit. I'm a peaceful man, you know? I wouldn't harm a fly."

He took a bite of steak and continued.

"I don't know who killed him, and I won't speculate. But Red was a weird, dangerous dude and he would lose his temper and get in fights with people, and he had guns up at his cabin, I know that much for a fact. My dad could tell you about that. But he was like a leech on the old man. Bernard was filthy rich, you know. And when rich people get old people latch onto them and if they're getting senile they'll start giving their money away. They get really gullible, and…it's just sad, what happened."

"So you and Hilda…"

"We're just taking it really slow and being really careful, because I'll tell you this: she's been followed several times coming up here, and I've been followed leaving her place, and I don't have anything to hide. You know, we fell in love honestly and she left her husband, and I'm sorry that happened, but she needed someone to turn to and I saw this person who deserved a lot better."

I was confused at this point, and my brain was addled with wine, and the sun was going down. He drove us back to town and I made him promise to let me buy him a drink the next time he came to Pirate's Cove, and he agreed, and he dropped us both off at the beach.

She stayed with me, which was nice. She seemed a bit lonely. She had an awful lot of free time to spend. She asked me if I had plans that night and I said of course not, but I might head to the Cove. We sat down on the beach and she pulled a picture out of her pocket.

"I wanted to show you something, this is crazy," she said. "Look at this picture of my family."

They were standing in front of a restaurant called Romanesco, which I'd seen in town. It was an old picture from the eighties or nineties. She was little, and her parents were standing next to each other, and there was what appeared to be an older brother standing next to them.

"This was before my brother died."

"When did he die?"

"When he was sixteen, just a year after this picture was taken. It was a crash on the coast highway. But I was looking at the picture and I realized he looks a lot like you."

"Really? I guess I see that a little bit…"

She held the picture up to my face.

"Yeah, he really does. That's really weird, huh?"

"Weird." This was great. Not only did she have a boyfriend but now I reminded her of her dead brother. You don't want to be in the brother zone. But once you're stuck there, how do you get out? She seemed more sad than usual that night and I felt a little bad for her, being stuck in this little town, away from her boyfriend, caring for a sick mother, haunted by her broken family. At least I was there to keep her company, even if I was trying to steal her from her boyfriend.

She held the picture up again.

"You know, this also reminded me of when we used to go to that place on special occasions and we would always see Sam Bernard with his son and the whole extended family. They were always there it seemed, having these big get-togethers. They seemed so normal and functional. Everyone in town loved them."

"But things changed?"

"Things changed. Things got weird in this town."

We were quiet for awhile.

"I wonder why bad things happen when you don't deserve them," she said. "Like why people make terrible choices or accidents happen or married people get divorced and all that." She looked at the ocean.

"The gods are strange. It amuses them to see us suffer, probably."

"Gods?"

"Yeah. I don't buy the one god theory. The universe shows evidence that there must be many of them, or none at all. And if there are gods, they obviously can't agree on anything. Some of them hate humans and some of them like us, and some of them are too busy to notice us. And together they all determine what happens to us. So that explains life as we know it."

"Might be true."

"It makes sense. Think about it. What do you think is up there?"

"I think there's probably one god in charge of it all."

"Hmm."

"And he just has a weird way of doing things. But he loves us."

"Okay. That makes some sense, maybe." My version sounded pretty harsh I guess. I wasn't doing a good job of comforting her. "I'm sorry to hear that about your brother. Must've been hard."

"It's okay. My mom and I are really close, but it kind of drove my parents apart. But we're all okay now. We survived."

We stared at the stars, lying on our backs.

"So now we have to find Red Simpson," she said.

"I was just about to say that. Do you know where French Canyon is?"

"I do. It's pretty remote. I didn't think anyone lived up there."

"Have you heard of him?"

"Yeah, he's a legend around here. He comes to town sometimes, you'll know when you see him. As a matter of fact…well, I'm going to a party where you might see a few people who know him."

"Really?"

"Yeah, tomorrow. You're free to come. It's a housewarming party for an old guy who used to know my dad. I try to stay in touch. He's a Wall Street guy who lives here almost full time now. It's kind of a huge compound he built. He's named Stuart Gold, he came out here in the eighties to buy a winter house and he used to hang out and get stoned with Red Simpson. This town used to be a lot more of a hippie town, I guess."

"I'm there."

That night after she left I wandered over to the Cove and it was pretty mellow for once in a long while. I got a Blue Mule, some kind of a cross between a Blue Hawaiian and a Moscow Mule, with a pile of fresh ginger shavings dropped in and muddled with lime, pineapple and sugar, then shaken with curacao, vodka, rum, and some mysterious syrup. At least that's what I think was in it. It was served in a hurricane glass and it was tasty, I will tell you. Not much happened that night but I overheard Dave telling someone, "You know how much he charged me? One dollar."

"That was your rent? So what now?"

Dave shrugged. "Lots of legal issues. We'll see."

The day had kicked my ass. I walked home and slept it off. I thought about Joe Duquesne and wondered if I should call him. I decided to hold off on that. I didn't know this town well enough. It was hard to trust anyone.

8

The next morning I got some coffee at Playa Roasters, flirted with Anna a little too obviously, and decided to walk around the town. It was an exceptionally sleepy morning and I started to see how strangely undeveloped this city was. There was an original, authentic quality that was rare in beach towns in California. Once you left the downtown, you walked through neighborhoods of small beach cottages with yards overflowing with flowers that grew in abundance from the constant sea mist and the long sunny days. I crossed the train tracks and remembered that the Coast Starlight went through here on its way down to San Diego. I had taken the trip once with my mom. I came to a park where a farmer's market had just set up. As I walked through I saw peaches, strawberries, local honey, grapes, and all the requisite leafy greens. It hadn't filled up yet, and there were just a few neighborhood people ambling through with grocery bags. Seagulls flew around, honking loudly in the morning air.

In the distance I saw the bell tower of the old mission, so I walked down the street to see it for the first time. It was an old crumbling, magnificent structure from the 1780's that was open for tours daily. Looking in I could see an enormous square yard with a huge fountain full of lilies. Olive trees and orange trees were scattered throughout the place. Around the mission was an historical district that seemed to be old adobe houses from the 1800's which were still inhabited. The people starting their day and watering their little gardens and walking down the streets and cooking breakfast (which smelled like tortillas frying in lard) were all short, dark Mexicans and looked like descendants of the original inhabitants. This town was living, breathing history. The unforced authenticity was unlike anything I'd seen. I'd been so enraptured with Pirate's Cove that I hadn't noticed these other neighborhoods. The air smelled like ocean, sage, eucalyptus, and burning firewood. These were probably the same smells you would have noticed in the 1790's when the missionaries were here. There was a continuity. The sprawl hadn't gotten here. The freeway was a mile away from town and it was over a hill, and there was no Target and no mall. Something amazing had preserved this place, but it wasn't precious or quaint like some beach towns I'd seen. There were local drunks, poor fishermen, old hippies playing electric guitar in their garages, hermits, Mexican neighborhoods where people kept chickens in their backyards. Sure, there were artists who sold their vases or landscape paintings at art fairs and had little galleries in town. You could get an artisanal cup of pour-over coffee here. That was a basic human right – it wasn't a first world luxury. And neither were those drinks at Pirate's Cove. There was no reason poor people in Cuba or the Pacific Islands or any tropical part of the world couldn't throw together those ingredients: a bit of lime, some sugar, some pineapple, and some of the local rum. Those things just grew in their backyards. Of course Pirate's Cove was a simulacra of something that had never been authentic in the first place, namely the post-war Polynesian craze that had occurred in California under the booming fifties economy. But somewhere in the kitsch was authenticity, because it was pure. It hadn't become corporate yet. Those drinks were mixed in earnest.

What makes places authentic? I wondered, walking through town, crossing the Santiago River into another little ramshackle neighborhood. Why was, say, Newport Beach so phony while East LA was so real? Well, Newport Beach was trying too hard, putting on too much of a show. It was created, like the rest of Orange County, by corporate developers in an inorganic way. It was created to resemble affluent regions of the East Coast or Europe. East LA was just cobbled together by working people. There were old Jewish cemeteries, and countless little, human-sized restaurants, auto body shops, tortillerias, street vendors selling everything. When you got a meal in East LA, it was made with love, and it was handmade right in front of you.

The beachfront in a shitty beach town is a travesty of corporate interests. The restaurants are enormous, there are too many of them, and they are designed not to provide good food but to serve a large amount of people. These beach towns are meant to cram people in, make them spend money, and then make them go home and leave the residents alone. They are Vampire Towns. Let's just call them that. They suck you in, suck your money out of you, and then usher you out at the end of the night. They are quite effective at doing this.

At some point in my rambles I came back towards the downtown and walked past Romanesco. I had forgotten that I needed to go there. Maybe one of the old-timers would remember the days when the Bernard family had gone there. It looked like a place where cops and city hall people went. People here would know things. It wasn't open yet but I would return.

Later that night Anna was driving me and her high school friend Scott to the party, and the road winded up through the hills outside of town. At the edge of town she slowed down several times to show us several big fields with fences around them.

"See this?" she said. I looked and saw SOLD signs on opposite sides of the road. There were PRIVATE PROPERTY signs hanging from the fence at fifty feet intervals. They were both huge swaths of land.

"Just thought you'd be interested," she said. "These just sold. They were always vacant before this. It was open space. My mom used to take me hiking up here."

"Changes happening in town," Scott, who had been silent, said in the back seat.

The party was at Stuart Gold's newly built compound, which was rustic chic and overlooked the canyon leading down to the town. There were magnificent views of the surrounding area. It was a rustic party indeed, mostly for neighbors and his local friends. He gave Anna a warm welcome, asking about her father, and shaking hands with Scott and me. He got us a couple of beers and showed us to the bar where we could help ourselves. Out in the yard, by a big fire pit, about twenty people were scattered around, and a fat guy was grilling what smelled like carne asada and making tacos for whoever wanted one. When there was finally a break in the conversation with our host I mentioned that I was new in town and curious about the locals. For instance, who was this Grover Simpson character I'd heard so much about? What was his story?

"Red," he said, shaking his head. "Where do I start. Well, I met Red when I moved here in the eighties, okay, and he was weird *then*. But as he got older he's gotten even weirder. The thing with Red is that he thinks there's treasure buried in the hills, and he's spent his life trying to find it. The history of this comes from an Argentinean pirate named Orozco, Luis Orozco I think, who came up and down the coast in the 1800's robbing all the Spanish settlements of all their riches. So he spent years in Mexico, Baja, and all the way up to San Francisco robbing missions and mining settlements, wherever he could find. Whatever the Spanish had stolen from the Mayans, he stole for himself. And the story is that as the Spanish army was closing in on him, he was right off the coast here, and he came up into these hills and buried it all somewhere, and they caught up with him near Monterey and boarded his ship and executed him. They never found the stuff he'd stolen. It's reported to be worth a hundred million dollars in today's money, something ridiculous like that. The thing is, though, some of Orozco's men escaped and some were pardoned, and several of them went on to give differing accounts of where the treasure was hidden. So Red has spent virtually his whole life researching this stuff, and digging around in the hills. He even built a cabin up there so he could be closer to the gold. But he still lives in town sometimes. You'll see him walking around. His house is on the old Bernard ranch property. It used to be the horse stable back when it was a ranch."

He paused. I was captivated. The orange glow of the flames periodically lit up Stuart's face. He had been looking up into the hills as he spoke.

"I heard he was friends with Sam Bernard," I ventured.

He nodded sadly.

"That was unfortunate, you know. Sam was a really great guy, a smart businessman, and the most loyal friend you could ever have. The thing was, he was a romantic, and he was gullible. He wanted to keep this town the way it's always been. He had this respect for history. He didn't want this town to turn into Carmel. But he could be obsessive, and Red had him convinced that he knew where Orozco's treasure was buried, but he just needed money to keep digging. So Sam started funding him and pretty soon they were both convinced they knew where it was. You know, a week or two before he died Sam came over here and he told me, 'Stu, we've found the stuff. We know exactly where it is. I can't let anyone know the location, and I can't even let people know I've been looking for it. Because people will do anything for that information.'"

"Did you believe him?"

"I don't know. He seemed to think it still needed a lot of work to get to the site. He said it was buried deep underneath the ground and you needed a lot of people to get it out, but you couldn't bring a bunch of people up there to help you because you can't trust anyone. Part of me believed him. He had a mixed reputation in this town, but he wasn't the cynical businessman people make him out to be. There was an idealist there, a romantic idealist. You know, he was just a hippie when I first met him here."

"So you came here when?"

"Oh, that must've been nineteen eighty…five, I guess. I'd made a lot of money in stocks out in New York and I wanted a getaway, so I bought my first ranch for almost nothing. And I made friends with him quickly, because he was my neighbor and he was from this old family who'd lived here for five generations. And he started getting into real estate and it just boomed in the eighties, and he was just a natural. I don't know. It's a shame." He shook his head. "You guys need refills?"

We did. We all went to the bar and he left us to greet some new arrivals. At some point that night Anna was on her phone in the driveway, talking angrily away from the other guests. When she came back she was upset and wiping away tears. Boyfriend problems. I had bigger problems on my mind though. This case was getting more complicated. Did Red Simpson have something to do with the murder? I just didn't know enough about him. He would be my next Person of Interest. Uncertainties are torture, I tell you. They keep you awake, they tease you, they take your mind on awful roller coasters through the night. Red Simpson just might hold the key to this murder.

9

The next day at Pirate's Cove I ordered the Orange Swizzle, a seasonal drink (when the local oranges were ripe) with aged rum and the house bitters and a cinnamon syrup and some other mystery items. I asked Dave if he knew Red Simpson.

"Oh yeah, he comes in sometimes."

"What? Have I ever been here when he's been here?"

"Maybe, once or twice."

"I don't remember any red-haired old guys coming in here."

"Oh, he doesn't have red hair anymore. What's left is all white. I'll point him out to you next time. I'll warn you though, he's not much of a conversationalist."

"What's he like?"

"Oh god, he's just an old nut. All he cares about is buried treasure, ancient curses, ghosts and goblins."

"He was a friend of Sam Bernard?"

"Yeah, I used to see them together all the time. Sam would drive Red around town in his big old Thunderbird. I don't know how Red survives without Sam around. Although I suppose his pension is enough for him."

"Pension? What did he do?"

"He worked for the county. He was an engineer for the water department."

I didn't really taste the rest of my drink. I just sat there, staring out at the ocean. The waves were dark and relentless. My mind was turning, turning. I had to go to Romanesco. I had to keep coming back here too.

The next day Anna was on my boat with me and we were smoking a joint. At some point she went inside the cabin to do something with her cell phone and I was lounging outside, playing an old Grateful Dead tape on my boombox as the wind blew gently in from the sea. I began to hear a familiar, disembodied voice coming from her phone. I went inside and saw that she was watching old videos of my dad on YouTube. I had told her about him earlier. Here he was on CNN, here he was in court, there he was giving a press conference for a football player he was defending who was accused of rape. We sat for a long time watching this strange footage from another world.

I said that this was a mystery story, and reader, I may have lied without realizing it. Now I see that in some measure this story is an elegy for a man I barely knew. This was someone I could have known in an alternate series of events. If my parents had stayed together, if I had chosen to live with my dad, if he had been more serious about doing the "dad" thing. It takes someone else to reveal these things to you. But you can't live in the world of might-have-been.

I convinced her to go to Romanesco with me that night when some people would be around, and she grudgingly agreed. "It's terrible," she said. "I mean, the food is really bad. They haven't changed the recipes in sixty years."

I said that was fine. There was a certain glory in that. This would be an historical investigation. She shook her head and said again, "It's just really bad."

"There's a bar, right?"

"Yeah, but it's…"

"I'll get a beer, a glass of wine or something. We'll get some bread and olive oil. They can't screw that up. I just want to talk to some of the old timers."

"Oh, it's ALL old timers."

"That's what I want. I just want to see what they remember from the old days when the Bernards used to go there. The thing is, old timers like to talk, and another thing, old people love me. I'll just be honest, I won't try to be modest about it. Old people just trust me. It's something about my face, my overall demeanor, my energy…"

"Yeah, I wouldn't brag about that. It's not really…"

"No, I think it's something to be proud of. Do old people love you?"

"They like me. They don't mind me."

"How many conversations have you ever had with someone over 80? Did they tell you secrets?"

"Secrets? Did they tell me secrets?"

"Yeah, how many secrets did old people ever tell you?"

"Well…"

"Yeah, I didn't think so. You think it's easy? Well, watch the master."

We waited until the happy hour/early dinner crew would be there and walked the half mile through town up to the aging establishment. It was dark inside and there were no windows. The afternoon sun was blazing on the black exterior but the air conditioning kept the place chilly. It took our eyes a minute to adjust to the dark. All I could see were the red candles at every table. Sure enough there were old people scattered throughout the massive dining room having their dinner at 5:00. And much to my delight there were some people at the bar. We went there and sat down. Patience. This would take patience. An old white haired man in a suit was behind the bar. This looked like the kind of man who could make a martini. I just knew. I saw the shelf of vodkas and gins, and I saw the various brands of vermouth, some rare Italian brands, and I felt hopeful. I ordered a gin martini, dry. He didn't ask what kind of gin. I liked that. Just make me a good one, okay? I shouldn't have to tell you how to make the damn drink. Anna got a chardonnay and I hoped she would switch to something harder. She was fun to hang out with when she was drinking hard liquor. He made the drink and it was ice cold and crisp and clean, with the floral notes from the gin. A very good martini.

Anna told the bartender she used to come here as a child and she had good memories of the place. He nodded politely and we were getting nowhere and I didn't know how to get someone to tell me about the old times, when the big happy Bernard family used to come here. To our luck, one of the waiters recognized her and said hi. They got into a conversation about how nothing had changed at the restaurant and how the clientele was the same. One of the old guys who had been sitting by the fireplace with his wife came up to get a new round of drinks and overheard us.

"The Bernards don't come anymore, that's for sure."

"You used to see them here?"

"Oh yeah, they were here all the time. They practically lived here. Every time they got a new account or sold a new house they would come here to celebrate. John and Sam were a golden pair, I'll tell you that. Father and son. They couldn't go wrong. John made that old man a billionaire. Without John, the old man would've been fine, but he wouldn't have gotten the kind of money he did. He wouldn't have ended up in Forbes year after year. He would've turned into another old hermit hunting for gold and none of us would be talking about him so much."

"That's a shame the good old days are gone."

"Yeah, the company's still successful, but without Sam it's not the same. They still do well, that's for sure. I miss him, though. I miss him a lot."

"I heard he got into the paranormal, ghosts and stuff."

"Oh yeah. He had so much money and so much time on his hands. I felt bad for him, he got a little senile, he had that nasty divorce, and people started making fun of him for all the buried treasure and the ghosts. But you know what? The man was rich, he was retired, and he wasn't hurting anyone. And you know, his son was good to him until the end. A lot of his friends stopped seeing him, and he got a little lonely in that big house. But I always saw them together and it made me feel good."

"Any guess who killed him?"

"You know what? I'm surprised it didn't happen earlier. People knew how rich he was for twenty years. He told the whole world about his priceless antiques. And you know what else? The month that it happened, there were three other robberies on the coast. One was a jewelry store in San Luis Obispo, and a couple of houses in Santa Barbara, the same deal where they broke in and took everything and the owners didn't even realize they'd been robbed for a week. Some group of robbers just came and left. I don't think they'll find 'em. They're gone by now."

"So did you see Sam and John around together a lot?"

"Yeah, John took his father out a lot, they were coming here a lot. The place would be really crowded, you know, on a Friday night, and they would come in and get their usual seat in the corner. That's what kind of people they were. They'd been coming here that long. It was like they owned the place. Everyone would notice when they saw those two coming in, like a pair of celebrities."

We had a couple more drinks and I walked Anna home and then brooded as I walked through town, walking in circles around the mission, walking past bars and almost going in. I ended up at the beach in a black mood. I wasn't getting anywhere. I was wasting my time here. This murder was getting harder and harder to solve and I still couldn't let it go. It wasn't just a random break-in. I don't know how I knew but it reminded me of something I'd heard my dad say a couple of times. He told me that he just knew when his clients weren't telling him everything. I guess I inherited that. I wished I could call him and tell him the whole case. He would have it solved in a half an hour. I wondered if he would have been proud of me, of the progress I'd made on the case. I wished I'd made an effort to get to know the guy a little bit more, especially when I knew he was sick. I was just mad at him for a hundred different reasons and I was too dumb to realize I'd regret it. You can't forgive yourself for being unkind to those who have passed.

I would have to solve this thing by myself. Something wasn't right, and I couldn't let it go, and I was getting nowhere, and I was still attracted to a girl who had a boyfriend, and everything was fucked up.

Anyone could have killed Sam Bernard, but everyone in town had made up their minds and moved on. But how can you move on when you don't have the answers and the killers are still at large? What was wrong with these people?

10

The next time I went to the Cove it was another golden afternoon, the kind that makes you feel a little better when you're down, and somehow a little worse too. I ordered a rum old fashioned, which I'd seen him make before but never ordered. It was on my list because he used a special rum that he didn't use with any other drink. It was something from Idaho of all places, and it was a deep gold color and looked fantastic. I watched him make mine as the sun lazily approached the horizon. A seagull perched on the bar next to Dave as he made the drink. He squawked, as if in anticipation of the cocktail, then looked at me for a second, then walked down the bar and stole a pretzel out of a bowl, then flew off toward the sea.

Dave placed an old fashioned glass on the bar, poured the rum and the simple syrup, shook a few drops of bitters, filled it with ice, and stirred it until it was good and mixed and the drink was diluted just a bit. Then he peeled the lemon and the orange and rubbed the peels on the rim, then placed them vertically in the drink. He grated some lime zest into the drink. Then he placed a maraschino cherry ever so gently on the top of the drink and slid it toward me. At the front end you had the rum, which was smooth as a ten-year Highland single malt scotch; the lime zest was just subtle enough to be on your radar, beautifully balanced by the syrup. The lemon and orange peels were there, hovering in the background, almost testing your ability to detect the subtlety of flavor. The bitters were also somewhere in there, a pungent herbal flavor at the finish. I sighed. Gorgeous.

The bar wasn't too busy so I asked Dave how the bar began.

"When I was growing up my dad us all these stories from the war, about Guadalcanal and the battles he'd fought in the Pacific. But mostly he told us about Polynesian culture, all this stuff he'd seen in Hawaii and Guam and so forth. He told us about drinks he'd had with rum and fruit juice, and these were fruits we'd never heard of, you know, guava and passion fruit and mangoes and stuff. It sounded exotic to us. And it was his dream to open a Polynesian restaurant here in town. Well, he couldn't afford to rent out a whole restaurant space, so Sam Bernard's dad, Herbert, he offered to let him rent out the old fishing hut that was on his ranch. It was just a little place, and he didn't charge too much. The town was starting to get built up at that point, and the city hall gave out liquor and food licenses to just about anyone who asked for one. They wanted to build up the businesses in town and attract tourists. And this place was just too small for a kitchen, so he made it a bar. My dad bought a lot of the décor from an importer down in San Pedro, and some of this stuff my he brought back himself from Hawaii. See, Polynesian culture was very popular at that time. And my dad had been working on his cocktail recipes for years at home, whenever they had house parties, and he got a pretty good repertoire. The bar did well with tourists during the season and with locals on the off season, and we just survived. So when Herbert died his son Sam took over the ranch and he only charged my dad a dollar rent. It turned out he'd been down in the South Pacific and he had this passion for Tiki culture, and he came back with drink recipes, ideas for new ingredients, suppliers, and everything else. Now, remember: Sam never worked for this place. He never took a single dollar from this bar. He was a regular and he owned the building, although he never acted like he did. He would tweak the recipes a little bit and then they would get popular and then there'd be a new drink. When I came of age I didn't have much of a choice as to my profession, because I'd been making these drinks since I was fourteen, you know. I just grew up making these for my parents when they had parties, or when they were short a bartender one night, they'd bring me in and I just learned how to make every drink eventually. So here I am."

"So what happens now that he's dead?"

"I don't know. He always told me was taking steps to protect this place, whatever that means, but as he got more into his gold mining I didn't see him as much, and then he died. I've been paying my dollar a month to his secretary and she's been taking it, but she won't tell me about the future of the space. I even have some of his stuff in the basement and I don't know what I'm supposed to do with that. He was storing a bunch of his old books down there next to my liquor when he died. He had so much of it that he ran out of space at his house. But you know, he owned a lot of plots on the beachfront and in the neighborhood, and a lot of them he only charged a dollar. Some of the tenants were friends of his, some weren't, but that's just what kind of a guy he was."

The bar started filling up and I was lost in thought again. Thank god I had this mystery to distract me from more depressing things. After awhile, Dave came over to me and nodded at someone across the room.

"See him?" I looked and saw a crusty old man.

"That's not Red, but that guy knows where Red lives. He goes up to see him sometimes. He's a lot nicer than Red."

I nodded. I couldn't just go up and buy the guy a drink; he'd be suspicious. People didn't do that in this bar and he'd think I was gay or European or something.

I ended up circling over to where he was standing to look at the records. When the record was finished I put on a Herb Alpert album. It got a few favorable remarks throughout the bar. The guy who knew Red was talking to a guy and a woman and they had reached a lull in the conversation. The man mentioned that Alpert was a good choice and I said thanks. Then, I used the most reliable conversation starter I'd discovered at this bar: I asked them what they were drinking. All I remember is that the guy who knew Red was having a Singapore Sling, which I hadn't tried yet. I hadn't moved on to the gin drinks, I told them. I was still making my way through the rum. I told them I was enrolled in Tiki University and I was still a student of the cocktails here, and pretty soon we were all talking. I slipped in that I was curious about the town and that I'd heard there was a character named Red who fancied himself a bit of a gold miner, and that I'd love to meet this fellow if it was possible. The man and the woman looked at the guy who knew Red, whose name was apparently Ronald.

"Ronald, you know a little bit about our friend in the mountains."

The guy paused, took a sip of his drink, and luckily for me, lacked the better judgment that sobriety would've provided him.

"If you want to go up there," he slurred, "you have to look like you're hiking. Or birdwatching, or something. Because if he sees you up there, he'll think you're trying to find the gold. Which is rightfully his. Or so he thinks."

"And you go up there often?" I asked.

"Yeah, I go up there to barbecue and hunt pigeons with him. Sometimes I bring him groceries. Sometimes we just go on a hike. He hasn't shown me the gold, if that's what you're after."

"No, I'm just curious about who killed Sam Bernard. I heard they were friends."

"Oh, that's all you want to know? Then he'll probably be willing to talk."

He gave me some rudimentary directions to Red's cabin, which I wisely texted myself because there was no way I'd remember. The rest of that night was a nice mixture of lights and music and good company. I stumbled home and slept like a baby. A baby full of rum.

The next day I went to the bait and tackle store and bought some binoculars and a birdwatcher's book. I had called Anna and she was willing to go with me, so we met at eleven and she drove us up to French Canyon.

The hike was steep and rough, and the sun was hot and there was no shade. For about a half an hour the mountain seemed inhospitable and I couldn't believe someone lived up here. But soon enough we came to a flat meadow filled with eucalyptus trees. I followed the directions just as Ronald had told me and soon we were approaching the overhanging rock that looked like a giant nose, and then we turned off the trail and followed the sound of a stream, going up through an improvised trail. We crossed the stream, walked through some brambles, and came to another clearing. Up against a rocky hillside was the cabin. It was larger than I expected, a two story ramshackle thing that made you wonder how on earth he built it at such an awkward and unreasonable location, so far from civilization. A large wooden sign in the clearing said No Trespassing. Something moved inside the house so I gave Anna the bird book and told her to hold it up and look through it. I put the binoculars up to my eyes and looked through them at some trees. The door opened behind us and a jolt of fear shot through my legs.

"If you wait around you'll see a condor," came a reedy voice behind us.

I turned.

"Yeah, he's been flying around all morning."

"A condor? That's rare, isn't it?"

"Sure is."

I told Anna to look up the condor in the book.

"What I like about the condor, is they almost went extinct. But, like all good things, they came back. You'll see him if you wait."

I turned around. "Do you live here? We didn't mean to intrude."

He said nothing.

"Yeah, the longer you're up in these mountains the more you see that wasn't meant to be seen."

I looked around with my binoculars and tried to find birds, but really I had no idea what I was doing.

"Yeah, some things don't want to be found," he went on. "But if you're patient you'll find 'em. Patience. That's all you need."

"Are you Red?" I asked. He kind of grinned and muttered something to himself.

"I've heard of you," I said, walking toward him. "Were you friends of Sam Bernard?"

"God rest HIS soul," he said to the sky. "He knew something *was* gonna happen. But I seen it myself, you know. When I worked for 27 *years* for the Playa Santiago Water District never did we have so many problems like the last year before I retired, and never did we have so much water di-*verted* and spilled and so many wells wrecked by VAN-dals! Yeah, Sam knew something *about* it, but what I know is that someone didn't want the farms…" Here he began to cough violently. "They didn't want the farms to get any of it and they wanted more from the Oviedo Valley…" More coughing. "…not even in our district. I just figured it's time to retire anyway. Might as well get my pension, get out of this madness. I left just in time anyway. Someone wants all that water for theirself. In the middle of this drought. Insane. And my friend Sam…he had a curse on him, bless his soul. He was a good man but in his youth he did some things and he took some things from some places where he shouldna taken things from, in places where he didn't know the spirits and didn't listen to the people from whom he took 'em. But he knew things. I think he knew things. I tried to help him in his hour of need, but I…"

And just like that, he had gone back in his cabin and slammed the door.

We waited for awhile but he didn't come back, so we hiked back down the mountain. On the drive back to town we debated how crazy he was and what he could've been referring to. There was some sense in what he'd said, maybe filtered through years of solitude and the maniacal search for gold. But we'd heard so many theories that all sounded halfway decent that they were all blurring into a haze of mystery. As we drove to town I looked at Anna. She looked really good that night. She always looked good. I was lonely. I just wanted to take her back to the boat, kiss her and take her clothes off.

But I couldn't stop thinking about Red's weird monologue. What had he actually said? Apparently water was being diverted away from the farms and I had a feeling that someone at the water department was letting it happen. Was something being planned, some kind of development that would require massive amounts of water? Also Red had convinced Sam Bernard that he needed to make amends for stealing precious ancient art and angering various spirits. That's all I knew for now.

"Want to go to the beach?" I asked, and she said sure. We went to her place and she grabbed some towels and walked down there. It was a warm night. We walked by the Cove but it was pretty crowded so we just kept walking south. We were talking about something, I can't remember what, and I suddenly slipped my hand into hers and we just kept walking like that. She held mine and didn't say anything about it. We were just joking around about something I guess, but all I could think about was the feeling of her hand in mine, her skin against mine, and it was a big turn on because who do you ever hold hands with? Your best friend? Your mom? No. It's only the most intimate of relations that will share a hand with you. It's what it *suggests* that is sexy, not what it *is*. It's what the mai tai *suggests* that is magical, not just the sum of its parts. It suggests the vast Pacific Ocean, the beaches of Hawaii, the Caribbean, British naval history. It suggests something beyond the horizon. But as usual I digress. Here is what happened:

She held my hand tightly as we walked, and suddenly she stopped walking and turned toward me as if to say something, but she seemed to be bringing her face toward mine and reader, we kissed.

The warm wind was blowing on us, and the waves were mellow that night, and over at Pirate's Cove they were playing "Teach Me Tiger" by April Stevens, and I could feel in her kiss that there was a deep need, a deep and lonely feeling that had been building. Yes, I had been lonely too. I ran my hands over her body as we kissed, the way I'd wanted to since we'd met. Her hair was blowing over her face and she was beautiful.

"Want to go to the Cove?" she said. "I think we should be in public, or we'll do something we might regret."

"Yeah."

"Just because I still have a…"

"Boyfriend, yeah."

Everyone at the Cove knew. They just knew. They'd seen us together, they'd watched us become friends, and now they saw the glow on our faces. Dave even raised his eyebrows when we walked in. Come on, he was thinking. Are you kidding me? I know what you two are up to. Just get a room. What are you even doing here?

But the old gentleman didn't say a word, he just took our orders and she got a rum sour while I got the Singapore Sling. For me it was a movement forward into unknown territory. Each drink had to mean something to me, and tonight since something magnificent and strange had happened I was going to move on to gin.

When Dave gave me the drink he said, "Don't forget the modernism convention this weekend."

"Oh my god!" I said. "Is that this weekend?"

"It is. At the college."

Anna gasped.

"Chris is coming."

"Your boyfriend?"

"Yes. He's coming this weekend."

"Okay, we'll pretend we don't know each other."

"What am I gonna tell him?"

"What do you want to tell him?"

"I need to think."

We finished our drinks and left and she told me she needed to go home and figure things out. She was distracted and left quickly.

I didn't know how to feel or what to think. I just wanted her. I wished she had stayed with me instead of going home.

I walked down toward John Bernard's place and saw that the lights were on. The wind was blowing strong and warm off the ocean. I stood with my hair blowing wildly in the strange night, and John Bernard appeared in his living room. He was screaming. He was alone. He was rubbing his nose violently. He took something off a table and brought it to his mouth. He teetered on his feet as he brought a lighter to his mouth and smoked something. I couldn't tell what it was. He grabbed something off the table and threw it at the window. He grabbed his hair with both hands and shouted something that I couldn't understand.

I walked back to the boat. This man was totally unstable. I'd seen my parents have tantrums on bad days but nothing on this level. I stood on my boat and wondered how I would sleep with all that was going through my mind. Somehow the gin and the rocking waves soothed me into a slumber that was dark and deep and filled with bizarre dreams.

11

The modernism convention (ModCon) was at Santiago City College, spread out on their sprawling campus. It was just enough to distract me from the miseries of that weekend. The Airstreams were on the football field, and they were magnificent labors of love for the noble men and women who had bought them old and dusty and had put years of effort and hundreds of thousands of dollars into restoring them. Each gleaming home on wheels was different, a product of its owner's unique creative passion. Some of them were small and outfitted with just a bunk bed, a mini kitchen and a table, and some had actual bedrooms, a shower, and an outdoor patio area with a barbecue and awning. I wanted all of them. Some of them looked exactly like Anna's. Several times I took pictures with the intention of sending them to her but felt a pang of jealousy when I realized I couldn't. I spent too much time at the Airstreams, distracting myself. I fantasized about buying one and driving around the southwest with Anna. We could spend a week in Yosemite, a week in Palm Springs, head out to Havasu, then Grand Canyon for a week, then Santa Fe. Then Texas – no, maybe not. Then home. Looking around at the Airstreams I was reminded that this was the good life; this was what modernism was about. Living in a place of your own, a place that gave you dignity and freedom. It meant that aesthetics were important. Style mattered. It was the one thing keeping us from barbarism.

There was a big art exhibit in the quad by the library and I wanted to buy most of what I saw. There were artists from the Northwest to New Mexico, and they were all united by a certain stylistic impulse that is hard to define but easy to recognize. The images were signifiers of a hazy yet strong commonality that made me feel like a member of a much bigger group than I'd realized. There were paintings and photos of World War 2 pinups, those wonderful Bill Krisel houses in Palm Springs, now-defunct Polynesian restaurants from Orange County, vacation posters from the forties, old orange crate art from the Claremont Citrus Company and the Victoria Avenue Orange Growers Association in Riverside. Pictures of rows of orange trees with the snow-capped San Gabriel Mountains in the background. All these other people got it; we were all in love with the same thing.

In the auditorium were more booths: people selling bartending supplies, which I would've bought if I had enough room in the houseboat for a bar; furniture and interior design supplies; condos and vacation packages in Palm Springs; architecture books (I bought a book of Julius Schulman photos); t-shirts (I bought a Sailor Jerry shirt); and high end rum from a small family farm in Barbados. I bought a bottle of their ten-year aged rum, which was a lovely amber color and which maybe I would share with Anna on the b– then I remembered. She's with her boyfriend tonight. They'll be in her airstream together, talking about their future, making out. Taking off each other's clothes. Making up for lost time. I know how weekend visits are when you're in a long distance relationship. You spend the whole weekend in bed. My roommate in college was in one of those relationships and when she would visit he would listen to Jamiroquai loudly while they had sex, and the music not only didn't mask the sound, it kind of complimented it and made it more distracting while I was doing homework. The problem was I only heard him, and never her. She was a Quiet Orgasmer and made no sound at all, while he would blubber how much he loved her in between unearthly moans that sounded like they came from a deep sea creature. Then he would come out of his room in his boxers, grab one of my beers from the fridge, and eat peanut butter out of the jar. She would come out later and watch Maury Povich in the living room and he would go back in his room and futz around on his computer.

But anyway, I knew what they were doing this weekend. My stupid imagination filled in all the details. I bought just about all I wanted at the convention and was leaving the campus in a cloud of impotent rage when I saw them. They were walking through the Airstream exhibit, holding hands. There he was. What an asshole. He looked like an asshole at least. Well, I only saw him from behind. But he looked tall and beefy. Just another big white earnest American guy, in love with his girlfriend. He was probably a lot like me. Probably a nice guy. Jesus, I felt sorry for him. His girlfriend was skinny dipping and making out with another guy while he was in grad school. This was a girl who meant everything to him. He'd stuck by her through divorce, a death in the family, separation, probably an eating disorder. He'd probably been faithful, turning down girls here and there, Skyping with her. He was probably feeding her stories about coming back to Playa Santiago when he was done getting his MBA or whatever, and planning how they would get married and move to New York so he could be in the stock exchange. I don't know. That's what my overactive mind was telling me. I watched until they disappeared in the crowd and then went down to drop off my stuff at the boat. I needed a drink. I went over to Pirate's Cove but they were totally jam-packed. It was full of tourists – assholes from the convention. Goddamnit, of all times for them to be full. This was when I needed a mai tai the most.

I went home and had some of my new rum, which I would have to tell Dave about. It was pretty good. No, very good. Very smooth. My stomach warmed up and I started to feel better, sitting on the deck of the boat as the sun went down. I put on an old Jim Croce tape and sat there, wasting time. Bad bad Leroy Brown. Great tune. After awhile it got dark. A cold mist drifted in through the boats, inching its way along the water and crawling up the beach. Soon all the beach houses were covered in fog. It was thick and I could barely see the boats at the end of the marina. The lights of the houses became milky and diffused and the sound of the waves and the creaking of the docks were all I could hear. I decided to go on a walk. I wandered aimlessly down the beach way past John Bernard's house. The wind was biting and the waves were loud. I reached the end of town and stood there for awhile, contemplating the nothingness that was out there for thousands of miles. It was a world ruled by the sea and all her creatures. We didn't belong out there.

I don't remember how long I stood there, but I started to walk back, slowly, because I had nothing to do and I was in no hurry to get home to my empty boat. As I trudged down a deserted stretch of the beach I heard what sounded like banging from John Bernard's house. Then a man screamed, but the sound was muffled by the mist and the distance. Then I walked closer and as I approached I heard one loud gunshot. I stopped.

A second gunshot clapped loudly, and there was silence. And then I heard someone running down the street on the other side of the house. They were loud, echoing steps and they faded away quickly. I ran around through the narrow alley to the street. It was a narrow street and it paralleled the beach and dead ended at a wall next to Bernard's house. Beyond the wall was a vacant lot and along the street were mostly houses that were shuttered and waiting to be sold or demolished. I ran down the street to see where the shooter had gone and noticed that there were little alleys everywhere, some leading to the beach, some leading to the rest of the neighborhood. The downtown area was south of here and no one was around. A few cars were parked on the street and there was no traffic as far as I could see. A few streets over a car started. Then I heard some more cars driving over on the main thoroughfare, Ocean Avenue, and I couldn't tell where he'd gone. He could be at the beach by now, or he could be wandering through the neighborhood, or he could be in his car driving away.

I ran back to Bernard's house and walked in through the open front gate. Someone had been let in by the owners, apparently. The front door was open and I knocked and said hello as I walked in, but it was silent. I turned the corner and froze. Lying on the ground facedown, his head in a pool of blood, was John Bernard. In the corner, slumped against a wall, was a young blonde woman. She'd been shot in the chest.

I panicked and ran out to the street, then back onto the beach. I didn't want anyone to see me in the house or coming out of it. I was sure someone would hear the gunshots and call the police. They didn't need twenty phone calls saying the same thing. But as I waited I realized that no one had heard the shots; no one was on the beach and there were no neighbors. The sirens I was waiting for never came.

I went back in the house and took some pictures with my phone. I looked around. A couple of beers and were open on the counter. And a third drink on the coffee table, what smelled like gin and tonic. A-ha, here was something. A single paper had fallen on the ground next to the coffee table. I picked it up. It was an official document from Higgins Properties, an agreement between the company and Grover Simpson. It arranged for Simpson to deed all properties awarded him by the late Sam Bernard over to Higgins Properties LLC, in return for a perpetual annuity of $40,000 and tenancy in all currently occupied properties free of charge. There was a confidentiality clause and some other legal language. I took the paper and left the house and walked, shaking, back onto the beach. I panicked, wondering if anyone had seen me. Then I wondered if I had left any fingerprints in the house. I decided to put the paper back in the boat, then call the police anonymously and say I'd heard the shots and gone in and seen them dead. That way I was just the guy who found the bodies. That's not a crime.

I went back to the boat, made the call, and told them I couldn't say my name and that was it. They didn't ask my name and didn't keep me on the phone too long. I wanted to have nothing to do with it. I didn't want anyone to know anything. Maybe Anna – another pang when I picked up the phone to call her. I poured myself a shot of rum to calm my nerves, and waited for the sirens.

12

Of course it was in the Santiago Sentinel the next day. Front page. I was a mess, thinking about the murder, thinking about Anna. I was at the Cove that night and everyone was talking about it, asking me my theories. I had none to tell them. I was as mystified as anyone. No, I hadn't heard the gunshot that night. I was asleep at the boat. I was working on my Singapore Sling when Anna called. I jumped up and ran out to the patio to get it.

"He's gone," she said. "Are you around?"

I told her I was at the Cove and she said she'd meet me there. She needed a drink.

When she arrived she ordered a mojito. You could smell the mint and lime across the room. Man, that thing smelled like a garden after an April rain.

She was pretty downbeat. She had told him that she was tired of doing the long distance thing, she was a different person than she was six years ago, she wasn't as invested in the relationship anymore, and nothing about me. He had been feeling the same things and they pretty much ended it. She was confused and needed to take things slowly. It would take awhile to process all this. Sure, I understood. It sounds like a good thing for both of you, I said, sounding more like her gay friend than a guy who likes her. I mean, it sounds like you guys were drifting apart for awhile, and…she was crying. Okay. Alright, let's slow down. She went on the patio and I was embarrassed for bringing drama into the bar. I went out to console her.

We finished our drinks and left, walking on the beach. I told her everything that had happened the night before and it distracted her. She was shocked. I told her about the note and she said she had to see it.

In my boat she sat and read it, aghast.

"John was trying to get all of Red's land? I didn't know he had any. But what for?"

"Maybe Sam left Red some land when he died."

"So, the doors were all open, right? When you went in there?"

"Yes. No one broke in."

"So, it's almost like John invited Red over to sign this deal, and Red brought a gun, which is strange, but not unlike him, and when he saw the deal he flipped out and killed them."

I nodded.

"But also, we can't rule out some other things. John was into drugs and gambling, right? So he likely had some pretty big drug or gambling debts. Someone could've come to collect, and that paper just happened to be there. It could've been some gangster from Vegas."

"But there was no sign of forced entry," she said. "He wouldn't have let some hoodlum into the house like that. And you said they were having drinks, right?"

"Yeah, it was someone he knew. He was wining and dining Red, giving him a drink, selling him this weird deal that Red obviously didn't like."

"But where is Red now? Did he just go back to his cabin?"

"He should've left town if he has any brains."

"But where does an old guy like him go? His whole life is in this town."

"Well," she said, looking back toward town, "he lives just up the hill a little bit."

"We should check out his place."

She showed me where his house was, and it was tucked at the back of a long driveway up against the hills near Sam Bernard's place. We snuck up the driveway and stood in the dark but there were no lights on in the house and no sound anywhere in the neighborhood. It seemed deserted.

"Well, his truck is gone," she said. "So I guess that means *he's* gone. We'll have to go up to his cabin."

"The sooner the better."

"Well, I'm doing the morning shift tomorrow, but I can go when I get off."

"Good. Twelve?"

"Yeah."

We walked down the hill and she turned at her street to go home. I was left with the rest of the evening ahead of me, so I figured what the hell, I'll go back to the Cove. Who knows what I'll overhear. It was the only place in town where people actually spoke to each other, where you could get an education just by going, where people weren't staring at their phones or a football game.

It was a weird crowd, mostly couples flirting. I called it a foreplay night at a bar when it was full of couples who you could tell were about to go home and have drunken sex. In one corner was a lesbian couple, two local girls in their twenties who were clearly on a date that was going well. They both had a cute tomboy look. They were just so into each other. The world around them had disappeared.

So it was pretty foreplayish that night and I was alone without the girl I wanted to be having foreplay with, but you know what? I had arrived at a place of acceptance. It was *okay*. I was living in the first world and I had enough food and shelter and my life was not in immediate danger, so who was I to complain? I was maybe halfway through an Appleton 12-year special reserve on the rocks, which seemed like a good thing for a brooding guy to have on a humid windy night that felt like rain. The drink was golden and oaky and so smooth.

And then a guy with a huge backpack walked in. He was about my age but a thick beard and suntanned, leathery skin made him look older. He looked at the menu for a long time, like he was studying the gospel (an apt comparison in my mind), and finally ordered the Tequila Sunkist, which I hadn't realized was on the menu. I watched with fascination as Dave muddled three kinds of tequila (a reposado, an anejo, and something that had been infused with oranges in a big jar in the corner since I'd first set foot in the place) with fresh oranges and sugar. He then shook the whole thing, put it in a collins glass and took a Mexican Sunkist (the one in the big glass bottle) and poured it over the top.

"Whoa," the guy said when it came to him. He took a sip.

"How is it?" I asked.

"Awesome," he said, taking a dirty wad of cash out of a compartment of his backpack, which he'd set against the bar. He counted it and laid some bills on the table, then sat to enjoy his drink, apparently in disbelief that his luck had taken him to such a place as this. He looked around the bar, then out at the beach, and I saw the wonder come over him the way it had to me on my first time. It was nice to see first-timers.

"Did you just come from the train?" I asked.

"Yeah, I figured I'd get off here and find a place to crash."

"Where are you headed?"

"Up to Santa Cruz to see my buddy. I've been in San Diego for awhile."

The wind blew in. It smelled like it was going to rain. We had some small talk, and it turned out his name was Jordan, and he asked me what I was drinking, and I told him how good it was and since he sounded intrigued I insisted on buying him one. He was beyond grateful. This was a guy who seemed to live on the generosity of others, but was blown away and humbled when it was offered, refusing the drink at first. When it came he relished it, I can tell you. What a blessed life, I mused. He seemed to be without ego, without attachments.

So after some pleasant conversation he reached into his backpack, took out a big sandwich bag full of cigars and set it on the counter.

"These are Cubans. Don't ask me where I got 'em."

"Wow. Never smoked a Cuban before."

"You like cigars?"

"I love them. I don't smoke too often but I never turn down the chance."

"Do you want to go try one?"

"Yeah. I'm sure the beach is fine."

Dave, consummate professional that he was, had a cutter and a lighter, and we left our drinks at the bar and went out to the beach. We lit up and damn, it was a fine cigar. A strong, funky aroma with a gentle taste that slowly became more woody and caramelly, more sweet as I smoked it. And then Jordan began to talk. I smoked silently, listening.

"So I've always had weird nightmares," he told me, "and night tremors and stuff like that. My whole childhood since I was ten or something. And last year it got so bad that I couldn't sleep and I had a breakdown and quit my job and just left town and went traveling. I mean, I was pretty straight and narrow before this. I worked in the admissions department of a college and I wasn't really a hippie or anything. But I just realized that I needed a change so I dumped my girlfriend and started traveling. And it was in New Mexico when I was staying with this Indian tribe with an old friend of my dad's. I told this guy about my issues and he said I should go to this healer on the reservation. And this old woman, she barely spoke any English. And she told me through my friend that I had to be hypnotized because something had happened to me a long time ago that I couldn't remember, and that I needed to face it before I could get better. She hypnotized me, and pretty soon I had these memories, you know, and they weren't really like dreams or nightmares, but it was something that I had suppressed, that I realized I had actually experienced, and you know I was never into unexplained phenomena or anything, but in these memories I was on some weird spacecraft and these fuckin'…aliens were there with me. I just remember that they were studying my body, and I was naked, and I was like ten or eleven years old, and I was so scared, and I was crying and shaking, and their little heads and their huge beady eyes were just staring at me, like they couldn't understand anything about me. And then all these other fuckin' memories came back to me, from these different times in my life. They would find me in different places and just kidnap me and they would put me on the ship and do things to my body and bring me back. I think they knew I couldn't handle it if I knew what was happening, so they drugged me or something. But I think I've been more at peace since the hypnosis. And I've come to accept it. And I don't think they ever wanted to harm me. They just wanted to study me and learn about me. But I don't know. I don't tell too many people, because it sounds crazy. But it's there, in my memory, somehow. I didn't dream this shit up."

"Wow."

We smoked for a little while. I didn't know what to say. How do you react to that? Eventually I asked him what he'd been doing in San Diego.

"Body boarding. Seeing my friend Jed from college. He owns a tattoo parlor down in San Ysidro. But I met this one dude at a party who told me this crazy fuckin' story, which is part of the reason I actually stopped at this town."

He took a drag of his cigar and stared at the sea.

"This guy must've been in his forties. He looked like he'd been in and out of jail. He was a tough looking motherfucker, man. Tattoos everywhere. He just had that hardened look. You know that look. He was drunk as fuck, man. And he started talking about shit he's done in his life, stuff that got him in prison, stuff that he got away with. And he said he robbed a house up here one night, with like two other guys, and they took a bunch of shit out of the house and it turned out the guy who lived in the house was home that night. One of the other guys he was with freaked out and shot the old dude, and they took all this shit and left. But the craziest thing is they were hired to do it. The people who hired them told them everything, the code to get into the front gate, where all this cash was hidden, which valuables to take, and they had some documents they wanted these guys to find. They didn't find what they were supposed to, but they took tons of shit and loaded it into this van that showed up when they were done. This fuckin' guy told me all of this. What a trip. That's been fuckin' with me ever since I heard it."

I told him about the murder and that I'd been trying to figure it out. Jordan didn't know anything else about the crime or who had set these guys up. The guy had been really, really drunk when he said all this anyway, so some of it was to be taken with a grain of salt.

When we finished our cigars we went back inside and finished our drinks. He said he would find a place to sleep on the beach before getting on the next train in the morning.

As I walked home that night it started to rain and I got back to the boat house just in time to avoid getting drenched.

I was just getting into bed when I got a text from Anna: Hilda Bernard had been arrested and charged with the murder of her ex-husband Sam Bernard. They found her in a Best Western in Paso Robles after a manhunt of several weeks. I just knew she hadn't done it. She wouldn't have had the money to hire those guys to do that.

I didn't sleep a wink that night.

13

The next day I met her at twelve at the coffee shop and we went to her place, where we got in her car and drove up to French Canyon.

"Hilda couldn't have done it," I said. "It's just impossible."

"Something is seriously wrong with that arrest," she said. "They're just framing her."

The day was muggy and humid and the sky was cloudy. The hike was rough; I'd forgotten how steep it was. When we eventually got to his cabin there were several wheelbarrows in the yard and we walked up to look in the windows. There was one main room with a ratty old bed in the corner. Mining and digging tools littered the room. Dirt and dust was everywhere, and I had a feeling that he was gone. We walked around to the back and saw more wheelbarrows. We followed a trail through the thicket and wound our way to an old fire trail that led to the bottom of the mountain.

"He must've parked his truck here," she said. "These are wheel marks."

I looked and sure enough there were.

"Do you think he…"

"Took the gold and left?" she said. "That's what I would do."

"But where the hell was the gold?"

"Only Red and Sam Bernard know that."

"And a dead pirate named Orozco."

"Where would you go if you had just killed someone who deserved to die and you had millions of dollars worth of gold?"

"First Disneyland, then…hmm."

"Well, I'd leave the country, I guess. But what would I do with all that gold?"

"He's probably been planning this for years. He probably has someone who is willing to sell it for him, or someone who flat out bought it."

We mused on this some more and then hiked back down the hill. The weather was strange, like my mood. Cloudy, warm, humid, threatening rain. She told me that her friend Kristin wanted to hang out tonight if I wanted to help her entertain. Maybe we could just hang out in the Airstream and make cocktails? I was completely okay with that, so we went to the liquor store to get supplies. Kristin liked vodka and soda, and that's what Anna felt like too, so I decided to forego any complicated rum drink and just slum it with beer. We dropped the stuff off at her Airstream and I went back to my place to clean up and rest.

I ended up showering and falling asleep on the beach near an English family on vacation. The kids were building sand castles and the father was reading as the mother talked on the phone in a lilting, sing-songy voice. The waves were so soothing and the sun was so warm that I was soon sleeping off that hike. I woke up and went for a swim in the water. Ah, the sweet healing Pacific.

I did some reading on the boat, did some people watching, and eventually the sun started going down and I made my way up to Anna's place. She was just waking up from a nap and I helped her finish the crossword from the LA Times. Kristin came over soon after that, with chips and homemade salsa from her mom's garden. Her family grew avocados, tomatoes, oranges, you name it. I was amazed by this town. Everyone made things from scratch, grew their own food, ate fresh vegetables, drank local wine. Kristin was a pretty blonde girl who worked at one of the hotels on the beach. Her mom worked in the chamber of commerce and had mentioned big new changes happening in town. They'd been trying for years to get this town out of the 1950's and bring it into the 21st century and finally things were happening. Kristin couldn't tell us any more but Anna and I exchanged a glance. One more clue that would lead me nowhere. I didn't feel like doing detective work that night so I tried to ignore what she was saying and kept drinking.

That night was a blur: we played music, danced, played Jenga, and got progressively drunker. At one point we played YouTube karaoke with a bunch of eighties songs and we were collapsing in fits of laughter. And then, at around one in the morning, after Anna and I had been exchanging glances all night long, Kristin went to the bathroom and Anna was suddenly on my lap and we were kissing. When Kristin came out of the bathroom she said, "Whoa…I guess it's time to leave now."

We mumbled our apologies and Kristin stumbled out the door.

The next morning I woke up next to Anna in her bed. The bed sheets were on the floor. The breeze was blowing in through her open window. We looked at each other. Our clothes were all over the room. She was lying on her side and her legs were touching mine. The sun was slanting in through her window onto the bed. The birds were going crazy in the tree outside the Airstream, having some kind of territorial battle. Her bed was big and very comfortable. I suddenly didn't care who had killed whom in this town. And I don't think she did either.

We spent most of the day in that bed, without our clothes, listening to her collection of old records. She took me through her bossa nova collection with some Sergio Mendes and Joao Gilberto, then played some Stan Getz and Sinatra and a Mutantes record. Sometime in the afternoon I thanked her for a lovely day and said I should get back to my place. We kissed goodbye. She said she wanted to spend some time with her mom that night so we agreed to maybe hang out the next day. I walked back in a daze.

That night I went to have some hair of the dog at the Cove and I only saw one local, a guy whose name I didn't know but who spent a lot of time there. He was in his forties and I think he was in construction. He always ordered a Tecate and tequila and would sit there with a newspaper, eating salted almonds and commenting on the news.

I told Dave I'd heard about the arrest and couldn't believe it. He said, diplomatically as usual, that he was sure the police knew what they were doing.

"Damn right they know what they're doing," the guy at the end of the bar said. "Hilda was guiltier than O.J. and everyone knows it. She was a psycho. Anyone who met that woman knows that she was out of control. She had the motive, the means, the anger. Everything."

I seethed. If only he knew. If only half of the ignorant poltroons in this town had the courage to question the power structure, to think for themselves, maybe some justice would get done occasionally. It seemed like everyone was content to blame it on the "crazy woman" and get on with their lives. Dave tossed me the Santiago Sentinel and I seethed even more when I saw Joseph Duquesne's article on the front page congratulating the Santiago PD for a job well done, catching up with the dangerous and "possibly armed jilted ex-wife" and lamenting the death of John Bernard, whose murder might also be pinned on Hilda.

"So, what's gonna happen to Bernard's house down there?" said the guy with the almonds. "How much'll they sell it for?"

"Two million at least," Dave said, and asked me what I wanted. I ordered the Naked Surfer Girl, a big blue vodka drink in a curvy hurricane glass with two maraschino cherries on top. It was good considering that vodka is not my favorite liquor. It just doesn't seem to add any flavor to the drink. But what the hell, I needed to make my way through the menu, and they weren't all going to be home runs. That's the way a bar works though: you have to give the people options. Some people apparently like vodka. I don't claim to understand these people.

"I bet Hilda killed John too," the boor went on. "But I don't know why she would. But you know, I was also thinking that it could've been a gambling debt or a drug deal. He was such a fuck-up, that guy."

I was so distracted flipping through the paper and seething about this fucked up town that I hadn't noticed that there was a new guy at the bar, probably a tourist. He was a suntanned guy in a dress shirt and sunglasses. He had an earring in one ear and graying hair and he wore tight jeans. He looked like a music executive from the eighties. He gave the menu a cursory glance and said to Dave, "So, what's good here? There's a lot of stuff on this menu, I don't know what any of this stuff is."

Dave asked him what he was in the mood for.

"Ahh…just give me your special. The house special. Whatever, is it a mai tai or something? You have those? Sure, I'll take one." He stared at his phone and began texting someone.

Dave made the drink and I looked at the guy. This…this newcomer had the nerve to come into this cathedral of cocktails and behave in such a dismissive, casual manner.

The guy got his drink and sucked down half of it, shrugging. He turned to me.

"I don't know what's so special about it. I saw this on Yelp and they made it sound like it was amazing or something. It's not very strong. I'll need a couple of these things to get a decent buzz."

He inhaled the rest of it and asked for something stronger. I told him to get a Zombie 151. He did. Dave made the drink as he always does, with love and care, and the guy looked around like it was taking too long.

"Can I get the drink? Shit," he laughed. "You take this long to make every drink? It's gonna take me all night long to get hammered."

The drink came and he drank half of it, then his phone rang.

"Dougie! Yeah, man, how the fuck are you doing? What the fuck are you doing right now? Why aren't you getting drunk with me? Are you serious? No fucking way. Who is she? Just some college girl? Like, right now, as we speak? You're shitting me! Well, take your dick out of her mouth and get your ass down here. NO, I'm at this fuckin…what's this place called? Hey!" He snapped his fingers at me. "What's this fucking place called?" I didn't answer and he finally looked at the menu. "Yeah, the Pirate's Cove, it's on the beach. Yeah, not bad. Cheesy tiki drinks and shit. I don't know, why don't you come down and meet me?" He drank the rest of his drink and motioned to Dave for another. He dutifully made it. The guy kept talking to his friend.

"Yeah, I can't tell you about it. Listen, the fucking guy doesn't want…it's totally confidential. It's a huge fucking job though. I mean, this shit is bigger than the casinos we do back in fucking Vegas. They want…listen, buddy, listen to this: they want fucking wall to wall statuario white marble…30,000 square feet. It's really fucking expensive Italian shit from ancient quarries. I don't know, I haven't done something like this since…yeah, the executive suite, the one at Dubai. It's gonna be a huge fucking thing for us. I'm looking forward…"

During this monologue he drained the second zombie and motioned for another one. Dave didn't make it and the guy snapped for another, pointing angrily at his empty drink and holding it up.

"Listen, can I call you back, I'm trying to get another drink here. Yeah, come down to the place."

He hung up. "Yeah, another. One more." He held up his empty drink. His face was beet red.

"You know those drinks are pretty strong," Dave said, handing him a glass of water. "Have some water, huh?"

"Yeah, another drink, dude." Staring at his phone.

"Those drinks are stronger than you realize," Dave said. "Why don't you drink your water, take a walk on the beach, in an hour I'll make you another one."

The man stared at Dave in disbelief.

"Never coming here again." He stood up. "How much do I owe?" He opened his wallet and took out some cash. "HOW MUCH DO I OWE? Aw, fuck it, just take it." He threw a couple twenties down on the bar and stumbled toward the door. "Never coming here again. I'm going on Yelp,

I'm telling all my friends that this place is bullshit." He stumbled out the door onto the sand and turned around, holding out his middle finger. His face was a mask of red rage. "NEVER coming here again." I heard him mutter something about Yelp as he stumbled away on the sand.

Dave and I shook our heads as he scooped up the money.

"It happens," he said. "Comes with the territory." I was almost shaking with rage but the old man was amazingly cool.

I took a couple deep breaths to calm myself. It was like someone coming into your home and insulting your mother's cooking. I flipped through the newspaper to distract myself. I stopped when I saw an article about Higgins Properties. It was a Joseph Duquesne article. The new president had been named. He was named Chris Phillips and he was the former CFO who had been with the company for twelve years and was excited about the new position, while humbled and deeply saddened by the shocking recent deaths of his two close friends and colleagues the Bernards. Nevertheless, he said in his interview, Higgins would still move forward with big new plans and this was what "they would've wanted."

I thought about the asshole who'd just left. Who would need that much marble? There were no large building projects that I knew of around here. Maybe some local millionaire in the hills was building a mansion, someone like Stuart Gold.

Oh, who was I kidding? I could feel it: something big and insidious was happening, or about to happen in this town, and it was going to be bad, and it was probably illegal, and two people had been murdered and one innocent woman was going to go to jail, and it seemed like everyone was in on it and no one was supposed to question it.

I finished my drink and stormed away, pacing on the beach for awhile before having way too many shots of rum and falling into a fitful, nightmarish sleep.

14

The next morning I woke up with the worst hangover in the world to the sound of my phone ringing. It was Anna.

"Have you seen the paper?"

"No," I said, trying to open my eyes. My head felt like a piñata full of fire being attacked by angry kids with baseball bats.

"Come to the coffee shop," she said. "You have to see this."

I threw on some clothes and stumbled up there and ordered a coffee and giant glass of orange juice. She handed me the paper. It was on the front page. I had to read it a couple of times:

Higgins Properties To Build Resort In Playa Santiago

It was a Joseph Duquesne article. The resort was called the Villas at Playa Santiago. It was the product of years of planning, and it was thanks to the city council, the Coastal Commission, the chamber of commerce and all the efforts of many business members and the board of Higgins Properties, and of course the late John and Sam Bernard. How had they gotten the land rights? Sam was dead, Red was gone. Who owned it and how had Higgins snagged it all?

The article was continued on page 3, where I saw a two page digital layout of the resort. It was an enormous, gaudy nightmare. It covered virtually the entire beachfront, wiping out all of the old hotels and Pirate's Cove. It was to feature condos, a five star hotel, shopping, bowling, a movie theater, and an enormous golf course. Everything made sense now. The horror hit me full on. I looked at Anna in disbelief. In the picture, about three quarters of the town as I knew it was gone. There were housing developments where the old neighborhoods once were. These were big McMansions, row after row of them. It was going to take over the whole town. Only rich people would ever be able to live here.

I had to go to Pirate's Cove as soon as it opened. I left the coffee shop and walked angrily through town, my thoughts a dark swirl of torment. Everything made sense – I understood almost everything now. It was unstoppable, though. Why had no one tried to stop this?

That day was a blur, and I somehow passed time until 4:00. I brought the paper to Pirate's Cove and showed it to him. He nodded sadly.

"They called me today."

"What does this mean?"

"Their timeline is to start construction in six months. That means all of this has to be gone by then."

He waved his arm at the beachfront.

"Everything? All the houses, all the hotels, this bar?"

"They're starting demolition in a month or so."

"But didn't you say that Sam Bernard said he was making sure this place would be taken care of when he was gone?"

"He did. But he never told me anything else. I still don't know what he was talking about."

"He didn't tell you anything about this resort?"

Dave shook his head.

"The only thing we spoke about was…well, it was an old joke between us."

Dave went fishing around in a drawer behind the bar.

"I'd been asking him for years for the recipe to a drink he always used to make me when I went to his house. He made me leave the room when he made the drink, it was part of his whole mystique. He said there had to be secrets between friends or else things got boring. But a couple weeks before he died he gave me the recipe and he made me promise not to look at it until he died."

Dave pulled out an envelope.

"I never got around to opening this." He opened it and looked at it. "Strange." He showed it to me. It was scrawled in a crazy old man's handwriting.

Calypso Desert Island Punch

IN THIS COCKTAIL ARE THE ANSWERS TO ALL YOUR QUESTIONS

Two **H**alf limes, squeezed

Two **O**range wedges

Muddle with sugar

1.5 oz Appl**E**tons

1.5 oz white **R**um

Shake with crushed ice – but don't **chap** your hands, **man**!

Pour into martini glass, top off with champagne and you're home!

I gave the recipe back to him.

"Goddamn, that's how he made it," Dave said, shaking his head.

"Did you say Sam was storing a bunch of stuff underneath the bar?"

"Yeah, mostly his old books."

"Antiques?"

"Yeah, he said he didn't have room at home."

"You mind if I have a look?"

"Why?"

"I just have a hunch about something."

Dave led me down the stairs in the back to the dungeon-like basement, which was full of liquor and old barstools and assorted antiques. It looked like the basement of a demented old widow. I looked at the books stacked up in piles, covered with dust. These books were seriously old, and they were huge. There was a King James Bible from 1750, a first print of *Martin Chuzzlewit*, a copy of Coleridge and Wordsworth's *Lyrical Ballads* from 1890, and...ah, yes! It was! A dusty, massive, brooding copy of George Chapman's 1616 translation of Homer's complete works. Calypso...I picked up the book and opened it gingerly, turning the delicate pages as fast as I could without ripping them. The Calypso episode was in the Odyssey, what was it? Book Four? I laughed. How perfect, a rum drink named after the goddess who traps him on the island for seven years.

I reached book four. No, that was Telemachus at the palace of Menelaus. It had to be the next one. Yes, here it was, book five – a single piece of paper fell out of the book. Dave picked it up.

"*Dave*," he read. "*If you are reading this, I have passed on without a chance to do my duty. All the records of my son's briberies and crimes are located in the chest in this basement. The combination is 36 24 36. He is trying to do a horrible thing which must be stopped. I fear him.*"

There was a sound in the bar up above.

"I'd better go up," Dave said.

"Okay, I'll look in the chest."

I texted Anna that we'd found something big and she needed to come down to the Cove. Then I opened up the chest, which was empty save for a banker's box full of papers. I flipped through them. Emails, most of them.

Dave didn't come back down; he must've been with customers, because I lost track of time while I read, and read, and read. They were emails from Sam and his assistant, a woman named Laurie, to members of the board and various people in the community, some of whom I'd heard of and some of whom I hadn't: the police, the mayor, city council members, members of the Coastal Commission. It was the Rosetta Stone of the case. They were promises of bribery in return for assistance in pushing this resort through. They were acknowledgments of gifts received. It was everything. It was vast, more vast than I could have guessed in my naivete. Eventually I looked up, my head reeling, my eyes sore from the reading. The bar sounded full upstairs. I walked slowly up the stairs and stood before everyone. The place was full of regulars. I knew everyone there. They had all heard the news. I didn't know if Dave had told them what we'd found. Everyone stopped and looked at me. No one ever went downstairs except for Dave.

"Well, what is it?" Dave asked, behind the bar. I held the mass of papers in my hands. Anna had just arrived to see me come out of the basement and she looked at me like I'd gone crazy.

"I think I've just solved a murder," I said. Everyone stared at me in silence.

"What is all that stuff?" someone asked.

"Well, I hope you all have a minute, because this is complicated. But it just might save this bar."

"Spit it out, son," said an old guy with a Blue Hawaiian.

I began.

"What we have here in these pages is the story of two men," I said, waving the papers in the air. "A father and son, with two different plans for the town of Playa Santiago. One of them wanted to ruin it and turn it into the Villas at Playa Santiago, and one of them wanted to keep it the way it's always been, a crazy little fishing village with good people and a lot of history, which happens to be the home of the best tiki bar in the world. I'll start from the beginning, and it gets weird, so stay with me. About five years ago John Bernard starting thinking about building a huge resort in this town, wiping out three quarters of the old houses and everything along the beachfront, including Pirate's Cove. He knew the real estate potential of this area, like anyone does. Put some McMansions in here and suddenly you can kick out all the people who live here and turn it into a vacation destination for rich people. Take all the water rights from the wineries and the farms and put in a golf course."

Someone had handed me a mai tai. I took a sip and continued.

"It was going to be a massive project, a huge boon for the town. He knew there'd be a lot of opposition so he kept it hush hush. He started bribing city council members, the mayor, the water and power department, the Coastal Commission, anyone he could to get this to go through. And they went along with it. He had the money and the influence to do this, and they would all get huge benefits if it succeeded. They all helped him do this. The only obstacle was his own father."

"His own father!" someone exclaimed.

"Yes, his own father. Sam Bernard didn't want this monstrosity on his family's old ranch. The old man was a romantic, a history buff."

"That's true!"

"There was no way he would let these old houses get torn down, especially when his friends lived in them and his favorite bar was here. But the son wined and dined him for years, being nicer than ever. Meanwhile Sam started realizing his son was bribing people and that he was gambling and doing drugs again. He started keeping track of it, and he printed out all those emails. I have a strong suspicion that an IT guy named Devin helped him get these emails, before absconding to Mexico. But I digress. After awhile, the son was running out of money. He was getting desperate. He needed his dad to give him the land rights he needed so badly. And then, at some point, Sam showed his son proof of the gold he'd discovered with Red. He probably showed him some of the coins and some pictures, but wouldn't tell him where it was. They had a confrontation, Sam told him he had records of all his son's misdeeds and he'd better stop this resort plan or else he would release the records. At some point, to protect the land even further, or just because he only had one friend left in the world, Sam secretly deeded his land over to Red, his buddy. So: convinced that Sam had the blackmail documents and the directions to the gold just sitting around in his house somewhere, John hired some guys to go rob the place and find them. They were probably never supposed to kill him. But they ended up shooting him and robbing the place and they never found what they were looking for. Because all along, Sam had them hidden in his favorite place: this bar. John then bribed the cops and the Santiago Sentinel to blame it on Hilda Bernard. Desperate, he kept wining and dining the officials with the help of the board at Higgins Properties, who knew all about the bribery. But he was broke –drowning in debt. Somehow he knew that Red had control of the land now, and he invited him over to sign a deal that would grant Red free rent in his house and an annuity from the company for the rest of his probably short life. This was in return for deeding all of the old ranch, which he'd been given by Sam, over to Higgins Properties so they could tear it down and build the resort. John actually thought this would work. This is how high he was. Of course, Red walked in there, saw the deal, went crazy and shot them both. And now he's taken his gold somewhere far away and he's living in luxury with his millions. A gift from his old friend, who was done wrong by his own son. Somehow they got the land rights, or they're just saying they have the rights, since the owner is gone. But once everyone finds out about this, there's not going to be any resort. And Pirate's Cove will be here for a long time."

"What do we do with these papers?" said a surfer with stringy blonde hair. "We can't go to the cops or the paper. Everyone is dirty in this town."

"Well," I said, taking another sip of the mai tai, "I have one idea. My dad had an old friend at the *LA Times* who still keeps in touch with me. He would be very interested in this."

15

I should tell you about Ray Hodges. My dad had known him from college and they would hang out together during my dad's downtown LA days, when my dad was at the courts all the time and Ray was at the *LA Times*. The two of them would go to the Pacific Dining Car together to gossip and gripe about their families, local politics, who knows. I called Ray, which must've been weird because we'd only exchanged a few emails since my dad's passing. But he called me back later that day when he heard my message about a newsworthy item in Santiago and a huge trove of documents relating to local corruption. I knew he was covering California political news and it was up his alley.

"Aris, how are ya?" he growled into the phone. I told him some basics and then launched into an abbreviated version of everything I've told you already. He listened attentively, interjecting with questions here and there, mumbles of familiarity with various characters. Ray knew California, and he knew it well. When I was done he let out a deep breath. Knowing that time was of the essence, he told me he wanted to know more and directed me to overnight a copy of the documents to him care of the *Times*.

He asked me if I'd met any girls up there in Santiago (a lovely town, he'd been there for a wedding years ago). I said yes, I'd met a nice girl and he sighed.

"Good for you. I'm going through a fuckin' shit divorce, Aris. She's gouging me. I'm happy for you though. Just…Christ, make sure that she's kind."

"Kind? Is that the most important thing?"

"Yeah, but not just when everything's going well. Everyone is nice when times are good. Ask yourself: what is she like in the middle of a shit storm? Is she still generous? Or does she run for cover and let the shit fall on you? You know, when I married my wife, I was twenty-six, I was a young journalist and I was a Pulitzer finalist for a series on Guatemalan immigrants I'd worked on. I got an advance for my first book, you know, and we had plenty of money and I bought a fucking house in Los Feliz. *Twenty-six*. You could never do that now. But here's what I *didn't* do: I didn't stop to wonder how she'd be if things weren't so easy. It didn't matter to me then. Why would I think about that? She was gorgeous, she was starring on a TV show, my career was going well…but when work dries up or you get sick, both of which happened to us, or when you get busy with kids, well…"

"Yeah, I understand."

"I miss your dad, Aris."

"So do I."

"I don't have any friends downtown anymore."

I promised him that I'd send him the stuff overnight and he said he'd look at it as soon as he could.

Right after the phone call I went to get the documents, which I'd left in Dave's basement, and took them to Jim's Business Center, off Ocean Avenue on a side street, where I made a copy. It turned out to be more than 200 pages. I took the copy over to the post office and got there just before it closed. It cost me over thirty bucks to send the whole thing overnight, plus the tracking info so I could make sure it got there. It would be there before noon, they said.

I walked back to the Cove with the originals in a big box and when I got there it was half full and the first person to look up and see me was Joseph Duquesne. I couldn't hide my derision. Dave saw me and I gave him the box, which he promptly took downstairs.

"What are you, working for this guy now?" Duquesne slurred at me. He'd had a couple already.

"Well, anything for a free drink," I said, playing up the clueless hipster he probably thought I was. Dave came back and I ordered a mai tai, absent-mindedly, hoping Duquesne would leave. Dave made the drink the usual way, and of course it was good, but the place had lost its spirit. The crowd was subdued, bummed out. We all knew.

Duquesne asked how much he owed for his drinks and it was over sixty bucks. Christ, I thought, how many has he had?

"Well, this one's on Higgins," he mumbled to himself, taking out a wad of cash and throwing it on the counter. He wasn't even trying to hide it anymore? A couple of drinks and he just lets it all out? This rotten town. This rotten, stinking, festering wound of a town. I was bitter that night, my friends – these were the thoughts drifting aimlessly through my head, and the booze didn't help so I only had one drink and left.

The next morning I awoke to a thunderous crashing. I stumbled onto the deck of the boat and saw one of the old beach houses on the shore in the midst of demolition. The tractor had turned half of the poor old place into cinder. I wished I was a smoker. I wanted a cigarette, or at least something to do with my hands while I watched this beautiful town destroy itself. I paced on the boat, wondering when Ray would get the documents and read them.

It was a slow, miserable day, boring and anxious. It wasn't until much later that my phone rang. I was asleep next to Anna in her Airstream and the phone jolted me out of a dream in which I was being chased through an enormous city by government agents, running through labyrinthine parking lots and catwalks over bustling streets with men behind me everywhere I ran. Somehow in my dream logic I had thought that this was Playa Santiago in the future. It had become a corporate, urban monstrosity.

I looked at my phone. It was Ray calling.

"Aris, I've been reading this stuff you sent me. This is crazy. Listen, I'm gonna come up there. I've been working on a story that ties into this and I think I can get a few days off. I'll tell you more when I'm in town."

I didn't have time to say anything and I was too sleepy to process it. Anna kind of woke up and asked who it was. I told her that Ray was coming to town.

"Good, you'll have a friend to drink with," she said and went back to sleep. I couldn't sleep of course, but that shouldn't be a surprise to you or me at this point.

I looked at her sleeping face. She looked like a child. She was good, sweet, pure. I needed that. I was lucky to have her. I lay down and waited for the sun to come up.

16

When Ray showed up he was a little bigger than I remembered him, but he mostly looked the same except for a scruffy five day beard. He was staying at the Maconda, a weird little mom and pop hotel a couple of blocks from the beach. I met him there. His room was in the courtyard on the first floor by the pool. I knocked on his door. He opened the door, gave me a hug and told me he was glad as hell to see me. I asked if he wanted a drink and he said yes. I led him through town toward the Cove. He needed to see what could be lost, what the stakes were.

"You look good, Aris," he said. "You're, like, a *man* now. I think the last time I saw you you were still going through puberty."

"Yeah, it was awhile ago. It's good to see you, Ray."

I showed him the downtown area and the beachfront. I had brought him a copy of the Santiago Sentinel with the plans laid out in their horrifying immensity. He gasped when he saw how much of the city would be destroyed.

"Alright Aris, I'll tell you my plans," he said, stopping to take a cigarette out of his shirt pocket. "I made a copy of those notes you gave me, and I gave them to my partner Jimmy at the *Times*. We've written a lot of things together and he's going to study that stuff and decide what is publishable. But meanwhile I'm going to write something short, just 500 words on this resort. I'll interview some people at Higgins and some other people around town."

He lit the cigarette and we continued.

"My guess is there are people in Sacramento who don't know about this, or don't know the truth. I also need to talk to a lot of people at City Hall. Anything they say will be revealing."

We reached the beach and started toward the Cove.

"And then I have someone else I want to talk to, but he's a little ways away. I'll tell you more about him later."

He had a devious grin on his face. We got to the bar and sat down to get some drinks. He looked around, laughing.

"This place is great, Aris. This is the real deal. I didn't think they still had real tiki bars anymore."

We both got mai tais and he was blown away. "How does he make these things?" As soon as he started into his drink, he was on his phone looking up information. He went on the patio to smoke and make some phone calls.

Ray came back after several phone calls and resumed his drink. "Okay," he said, "I have a couple of interviews at Higgins tomorrow. I'll make some phone calls to some people in Sacramento that I know, and I should have this thing written by the end of the week."

"And who is the other person you were thinking of?"

"Oh. This is a guy that Jimmy says was connected to John Bernard a few years ago in a really weird kidnapping case. The guy is named Psycho Billy and he runs a meth empire out of a small town a couple hours from here. John Bernard was a person of interest, and he paid for Billy's defense, and the witnesses disappeared, and no one was prosecuted. I interviewed Psycho Billy last year for an article I was writing and he seemed to trust me. I need to talk to him because…well, when you're a reporter you get instincts and you learn to go with them." He took a sip. "That's all I can say. You're free to come with me if you want. Should be an interesting trip."

After our drinks we split up and he walked off to get a sense of the town. I told him to check out the mission and told him where to go. I felt better than I had in a long time. Finally someone with some integrity was here to sort through this mess. I called Anna and she was at her friend's house having a bonfire up the hill and I was invited. Did they need anything? Yes, they needed tequila and something to grill. Being a gentleman, I stopped at the carniceria and picked up some tortillas, salsa and carne asada, and stopped at Santiago Liquor for the tequila. I walked up there and shared a joint with her and her friends, then grilled up the meat and spent the rest of the night by the fire sipping tequila with her and her friends. It was a glorious California night. As we left Anna said she wanted to go to the boat tonight.

"Maybe we could get you a bigger bed," she said. "I think you'll be needing it."

"Okay. I could do that."

"I'll take you to the outlet stores by the freeway. There's a good furniture place over there. We'll measure your room and see, but I think you can fit a Queen bed in that room. And my mom and I were talking, and we think you should invest in real estate around here. She's does real estate and she knows some good properties that are a good deal right now, that you could rent out. You basically make free money every month. I mean, before you spend *all* of your inheritance on mai tais. Do you mind if I ask how much your dad left you?"

"Enough to pay for law school and rent for a couple of years afterward."

"That's a lot. Wow."

"It's one of the reasons I never saw him. Always working."

"Well…that is a lot of money, but if you're smart, you could turn that into even more money. Just something to think about, because…"

She went on. I loved this woman. This was stuff I never would have thought of. Maybe she would make a grownup out of me. My parents had tried for years with few results, but with Anna adulthood was sexy. We walked on the beach for awhile before going back to the boat. She was tipsy, the clothes came off easily, and afterwards we slept on top of each other in my little bed as the boat swayed gently in the water. She was right. I did need a bigger bed.

I didn't see Ray over the next few days but I got a few text messages from him saying that he was getting good material and this was big, bigger than he could have imagined. I went to the Cove a couple of times and hung out at Playa Roasters, drinking too much coffee, just so I could see Anna do her pour over and tip her a couple of bucks. The scene was pretty mellow up there. It was always a good energy: students from the college reading giant psychology textbooks and old guys talking about the drought, housewives meeting with their dogs or babies, professors from the college grading papers, fishermen filling up their giant plastic mugs before heading out for the day. People were usually talking about fairly civilized things: Carl Jung, Woody Allen's new movie, tantric yoga. They were sober, they were clear-headed. I usually saw a couple people every morning whom I'd seen at the Cove the night before, where they'd been singing a sea chantey or laughing until they were red in the face. But in the morning they were reading the paper, drinking espresso.

Anna and I were inseparable, and it was probably a good thing when Ray told me he was done with his article and he was going on the next phase of his investigation. I hadn't left the town in a long time and I needed a road trip, and with absence making the heart grow fonder and all that sort of business, I figured it would be a good idea to go with him.

We left in the morning after he'd written his article and made corrections, and it was going to be on the second page of the California section. It would take a couple of days, but it would probably be appearing on the website sooner.

He didn't check out of his hotel because he'd be returning in two days. There was a nice little hotel where we could stay while we were down there, he said, and it should be an easy little trip.

We drove away from Playa Santiago, south and east over the mountains, past almond and avocado orchards, and we listened to an AM station playing bluegrass while he told me what would be in the article.

"So first I talked to the people at Higgins, and they all said the same thing: 'We're so excited about this new project, this will rejuvenate the economy of Playa Santiago and the entire central coast, we'll have shopping, entertainment, et cetera.' There was one exception, someone who was way way anonymous. This person said that the project still wasn't legal, and that a lot of crimes had been committed by many employees of the company to force it through. That's all she said. I can't even tell you who she was, but that's her word. So then I talked to the Coastal Commission, and the woman there said the area has been zoned for this project and the Commission had known about it for years and it would be a good thing. But that's funny, because the head of the historical society told me that nothing is supposed to be built here, and that the state senate has blocked his inquiries into this. They won't give him any information. But that's not all; an anonymous source at city hall told me that John Bernard has bribed members of the city council in order to make this thing go through."

"Is all this going in the article?"

"All of it."

"What will happen?"

"It's hard to say. A lot of shit will hit the fan. But that doesn't mean the demolition won't continue. Contractors have been hired, wheels are in motion. This thing is gathering steam and at a certain point it will be very hard to stop."

"But when people see this article…"

"Sacramento works very slowly, Aris. It might take awhile for things to happen. But things will happen. I know this from experience."

I was somewhat reassured so I asked him about the gentleman we were going to visit.

"Psycho Billy," he chuckled. "Well, hopefully you won't have to see him at all, but this hotel or commune, whatever you call it, it's very nice. I think you'll like it. Very interesting people up there. Thanks a lot for coming with me, Aris. It gets lonely on these trips. But it's so fun, damn it. I don't care if Kelly hates me for taking off like this. I told her she has to take the kids for the next week, maybe more. But what do I have to lose? She already hates me."

It is what it is, I thought, and stared out the window at the almond trees. I was lucky to know him and grateful that he was here, so I couldn't judge.

17

It was a small valley surrounded by hilly terrain with a lake in the center, filled with little farms and orchards and hovels linked by winding pathways through the trees. This was a part of California I'd never been to before. A breeze blew through the valley over the lake and the meadows and bushes seemed to whisper at me. The "hotel" was a series of huts owned and operated by Mama Jane, a gray-haired, chubby little woman with a big laugh and several cats. I was in a hut that was next to the communal area, where people were sitting around a fire in the dark when we arrived. Ray went to his room for the night and I settled into my new home, where my bed was a hammock. I was exhausted and I fell asleep swaying in the air to the sounds of a crackling fire and the gentle chatter of the people outside.

The next day Ray went to see his contact, who lived in a compound up in the hills somewhere. I went to shower and it turned out there was one big outdoor shower area for everyone. When I got there an attractive woman was taking a leisurely shower, humming to herself. I'd seen her the night before at the fire. She looked at me and smiled as she massaged her head with shampoo. What the hell, I thought, and awkwardly undressed and got started. I felt a little better when an old guy walked in and started showering. Now it was normal, not just the two of us. Afterwards the two of them lay on benches by the fire area to dry off, where a couple other people were meditating naked. Since there were no towels at this place I was forced to do the same, and it took me about twenty minutes of sunbathing to dry off. Not a bad way to start the day, actually.

Mama Jane made a big pot of thick oatmeal full of peaches and blueberries, and a pot of strong coffee, and we all sat around having breakfast and I got to know some of the other people staying there. Nice people, really. A lot of them seemed to be long term guests without any discernible means of paying, but I wasn't judging. I was there to investigate a murder. Or hang out while my friend investigated a murder.

I wandered through the valley until I arrived at the lake where I sat and enjoyed the near total silence. I hadn't had this much silence in years. At Playa Santiago there were always the waves and the seagulls, but here there were long stretches of no sound. I almost couldn't believe it when a shepherd came to the lake with his flock of sheep. They had come from a grove of trees and they were now drinking at the shore. The man appeared to be a few years older than me and he had light blonde hair and a ruddy face. He nodded at me and gazed across the lake. After some moments he walked over to me and said hello.

"Are these your sheep?" I asked.

"Yeah. Thirsty little buggers."

"You have a farm here?"

"Yeah, we make cheese and wool. We trade with other people in the valley. We're up in the foothills. What brings you here?"

"I'm helping my friend investigate a murder. He's a journalist and he's interviewing someone who lives around here."

He took a piece of grass between his hands and blew on it, releasing a reedy blast that echoed in the valley. A few of his sheep raised their heads.

"What about you?" I asked.

"My wife and I came here a few years ago," he began. "I worked up in the Bay Area for awhile, doing tech. But the company I worked for, I started to see that they weren't trying to make the world better. They were trying to make it worse. Because that was the only way they could make money. And they were giving people's private information to the government and I was helping them. For a long time I didn't mind doing this. But one night I saw a news story on TV about one of the factories where they made some of our hardware, and it was this place in Indonesia where they make three dollars a week and they work 14 hours a day without a break in a factory without ventilation, inhaling toxic fumes. I kind of made some jokes about it, saying it was a lie or laughing it off. But a few days later I was driving to work and instead of going to work I just drove in a circle around the Bay Area, over and over. Across the Dumbarton Bridge, over to Fremont, up the 880 into Oakland, across the Bay Bridge, into San Francisco and down the Peninsula, listening to an old Sinead O'Connor CD until I ran out of gas in Chinatown at 8:00 at night. I called my wife and told her what happened and said that I thought I was having a nervous breakdown and I couldn't go back to work. My wife had grown up in a farming family and her parents helped us get this started. She was ready to leave the city anyways. Find a better place to raise our son."

He looked back at his sheep. The man's face was haunted, I tell you. He'd been through some kind of hell and was crawling slowly back.

I asked him what kinds of people lived in the valley.

"There's a lady named Jill who grows vegetables over there. Lots of leafy greens. She also has chickens and she'll give you all the fresh eggs you need. There's an old couple who grows oats and wheat and they have an old stone mill and they have a daughter with down's syndrome who has a little bakery on the property. And George is a friend of mine who grows avocados and oranges. And there's a weird guy across the river who makes herbal remedies and potions. He sells his stuff to a couple of bars. There's some famous bar down on the coast that comes up here to buy bitters and syrups from him. Pirate's Cove."

I almost gasped aloud.

"Yeah…I live down there in a houseboat. I go to that bar all the time. Where did you say he lives?"

"Who, Dr. Warren? Right over there. You can see his cabin from here."

He stood up and walked about twenty feet to the right. He pointed. The edge of the cabin was just visible. He called his sheep together and said he had to get back to the pasture. I thanked him for talking to me. I couldn't believe my luck.

That afternoon I walked over to Dr. Warren's with one last mystery to solve. Surely he would reveal to a curious stranger what was in his potions. What was the harm? This would be the final mystery, the last piece of the puzzle. I had wondered what was in those drinks every time I drank them. I had watched Dave pouring elixirs out of nameless bottles marked "#3" and "#7" and wondered, and wondered. With great self-control I refrained from asking Dave, time after time, out of respect, because it was an unwritten house rule. I approached the rickety old cabin with its yard overflowing with herbs and vines and I peered into the backyard, where more greenery was flowing out of pots and climbing up the fences. I paused.

Maybe I didn't need to know. Maybe I wouldn't like the drinks as much anymore. Had I ever enjoyed a magic trick more after knowing how it was done? No! When I watched the video explaining how David Copperfield levitated over the Grand Canyon the trick became stupid, infantile!

With great doubt and what I considered to be great maturity, I turned and walked away. I don't really regret it that much either.

I talked to Anna on the phone that afternoon and told her that we'd have to come back here together sometime because this place was a trip. She'd never heard of it before. She said that we needed to hurry up because they'd bulldozed two more buildings on the beachfront and she'd seen even more detailed plans for the resort and the thing was hideous. She told me to imagine the Hearst Castle as redesigned by Liberace and Donald Trump, with IMAX movie theaters, a Planet Hollywood, a Hard Rock Café, and every other bad chain restaurant she had ever heard of. The streets in the town would be renamed "Via Bella" and "Via Roma" and the villas were called The Tuscany, The Fontainebleau, The Versailles, The West Hampton, etc. There were clubs with bottle service. A high end tattoo parlor. A B-list rapper was in talks to create a Club 54 reboot with his name on it. Okay, I told her, I would try to hurry, but Ray was AWOL and I didn't know when he would return.

That night I sat around the fire with the other residents. We were all drinking some weird hooch mixed with fresh lemon juice and local honey, which was delicious. Some guy brought out a guitar and the lady who ran the place brought out her bongos, and an old guy suddenly appeared with an oboe, and it became a jam session. A guy about my age with dreadlocks produced a bunch of bison steaks for us to grill. "My buddy has a bison farm in Montana," he shrugged. "I just came from there." We grilled them over the fire and had them with some roasted corn.

That night I woke up with a demonic headache and I stumbled out of the cabin to go piss. I walked past someone's cabin and the door was open and a candle was lit. Two middle-aged women were having sex. One of them said hi to me. At this place it wouldn't be strange for me to go in and ask for an Advil, and for one of them to get up, give me one, and resume making love.

The next day I was completely blasted from whatever the hell I'd ingested the night before. I shunned the light of day and drank well water, cursing myself and Ray for bringing me here and disappearing. It was sometime in the afternoon when Mama Jane showed up at my door. I looked up at her from my bed.

"You're Aristotle, right? There's a guy here who says your friend is in trouble. You want me to show him in?"

I nodded and felt a shiver of doom overcome me.

18

He was Hispanic, in his mid-thirties, a bit shorter than me, and very worried. He spoke English very quickly with a thick accent.

"I'm so sorry, so sorry about what happened, but your boss tell me to come and see you if anything happen. Something happen to him, I can't say, I think I know about it, the place where they take him. I working with Psycho Billy many years, sometime he do things crazy, most time he's good and I help him with many things. This time he have too much, he take your boss."

The poor guy was sweating. Was he on something?

"Something happened to Ray? Where did they take him?"

"Ray, yes, Ray, they take him."

"Where?"

"You come."

I sat up.

"Okay, I need to put some clothes on."

He stood in my room while I looked around for my pants and my wallet and everything else, and he paced across the floor while I got ready. I drank two big glasses of water and followed him outside.

It was an old Toyota pickup truck with the cover on the back. I got in and we were driving through winding mountain roads towards the vastness of the high desert. The sun blazed horridly ahead of us as we descended into the badlands. He wiped sweat from his brow and turned on a Mexican Christian radio station. All I could understand were *salvacion, Jesucristo, infierno, diablo*. He was fighting off sleep and shaking his head and slapping his face to stay awake, and at one point he stopped at a truck stop. He took a bag out of the glove box and left. He came back drinking a can of Coke, put the bag away, and took off. He was focused on the road from that point on. As the sun set behind us we sped down the empty highway in the fading desert light. The heat was still oppressive. He took several phone calls and spoke rapidly in Spanish.

I was fighting the urge to sleep and my hangover hadn't improved. I realized I didn't know his name and asked him.

"Guillermo."

There was a silence.

"Billy go too far when he have fun, and then…you don't know what is going to happen."

"Where are we going?"

"Some farther. He take your friend and your friend will not be okay if he spend too much time, and then he will be in trouble. Everybody like to have fun with Billy but he can…make you do thing. He can tell you to do something and you will do this thing, because you think it's maybe a good idea, but later you don't know what happen. I see this, many times."

We stopped for dinner at a little Mexican place and sat in the car eating huge burritos filled with carne asada, beans, rice, cheese, guacamole, and incredibly spicy salsa. After that, and an ice-filled Coke in a Styrofoam cup, I started to feel like a human being again. The desert wind was cool now, and it felt nice blowing into the car. Guillermo was playing some kind of Mariachi music that sounded like a psychotic mantra they would play on repeat in hell.

Finally we arrived at what appeared to be a cheesy bar in a small desert town off the freeway near a bunch of onion fields. The sign outside was neon, and it flickered on and off in purple and orange: Punchy's Saloon. God.

Guillermo knew the guy at the door and they exchanged some words in Spanish. It was almost pitch black inside except for the red candles at the tables. The place was half full of well-dressed Mexicans. A Mexican group was onstage playing the same exact music I'd been listening to ad nauseam in the car. I needed a drink, so I asked Guillermo if we had time for one. "Yes," he said.

He got a Tecate, and I ordered two shots of expensive tequila and a glass of water and paid for everything.

"We go downstairs," he said. I followed him down a hallway past the bathrooms and the kitchen to a door, where a fat Mexican guy who also knew Guillermo exchanged more words. We went downstairs.

It was a goddamn brothel. There were a bunch of areas separated by red curtains where middle aged white guys were having sex with these…white women? Euro-disco music was playing, and incense was smoking, and I heard languages that I didn't understand, and…I looked around. These were very attractive women. They were doing everything imaginable with these men. There were threesomes, there were simple blowjobs, there were men tied to chairs getting slapped in the face. I listened while Guillermo roamed around in the dark, bumping into things, looking for Psycho Billy and Ray and calling out to them in broken English. I looked and listened some more. The whores were *Russian*. All of them. One of the girls came by with a tray of shots and offered one to me. I grabbed it and thanked her, and Jesus she was hot…she was wearing nothing. Her crotch was unshaven, and that was nice, I thought as I took my shot, to see a woman in the sex industry whose vagina actually looks like it belongs to an adult…and then the shot was going down easily, and it was minty and kind of spicy, and I started wondering what was in it, when my stomach started twisting, and in about two minutes I was basically tripping balls.

I remember Guillermo coming out of a room with Ray, who was having an argument with a man I took to be Psycho Billy, and Ray was begging Guillermo to do something, and holding the prostitute by the arm and trying to take her towards the door. Guillermo was protesting and I was laughing on the floor. And then we were running up the stairs and out the back door, and the bouncers were chasing us because this prostitute was now coming with us, and we all jumped into the truck as gunshots started sounding. Ray was singing *Guantanamera* while we ran for our lives.

The night air was blowing in and the desert was dark. Ray was in the back with the woman.

"She's coming with us," he told me through the partition. "I'm clear-headed, we're both very clear-headed about this. I've been drugged, but this is not about that."

As he spoke I tried to follow what he was saying. I was still high. Whatever they'd given me made me want to take off my clothes and grope someone. In my hallucinations I thought the night air tasted purple. I looked back at the Russian. She was beautiful. She was sleeping in his arms. He spoke on.

"I don't know what the two of us will do, but we'll figure that out. Listen, Aris, we have to go back to Billy's place. I left my materials there, all my notes and recordings. I have enough for the articles. He was selling drugs to John Bernard, but listen: Billy is a very convincing person. He takes you under his spell, he convinces you to do things. He was using Higgins as a tax haven, he was bribing John Bernard. He was helping to finance that resort with drug money. He still is. But here's…Aris, you need to listen to this: he was using John Bernard as a sex slave."

"What?"

"It was an s and m thing they did. They would get high and Bernard would be his slave. And Psycho Billy took pictures of all of this. He offered to pay off Bernard's gambling debts, all of this stuff, but in return Bernard was a sex slave, he bought drugs from him, brought him new clients, got him involved in this resort."

"Do the cops know about Psycho Billy? Why isn't he in prison?"

"They've been investigating him for a couple years. Aris, they're building a case, they're putting it all together. I don't know how much I can say in this article, I'll have to talk to my editor. A lot of this was off the record. But we have to…"

I looked back. He was asleep.

19

We got back to the hotel and I went straight to bed. I didn't know what time it was. When I woke up a cat was on my bed meowing at me. It was full daylight. I walked to the well to get a cup of fresh water, went to take a piss, and walked past the showers. Ray and his Russian were showering in there.

"Oh, hey, Aris!" he said. He didn't seem hungover. She said hello to me. I understood what he saw in her. She was the kind of prostitute you'd want to save, if ever there was one.

"One more thing," he said as I tried to walk away. "You thought that Red Simpson killed John Bernard. He didn't."

"What?"

"Psycho Billy did it. He flew into a rage one night during one of their arguments and did it. He just flat out told me. But John did kill his father. He hired a bunch of goons to do it. But it was Psycho Billy's idea, and he paid for it. You basically solved the whole case without me, Aris. I'm impressed."

"Thanks," I said, looking away from his large naked body. "I have a hangover and I need to process this." I walked away and went back to sleep for two more hours. That afternoon he drove back to Billy's place to retrieve his notes and his tapes and came back with a big bag of evidence. I was relieved to see it all. I told him what Anna had told me about the demolition, and tried to communicate the urgency of the issue.

The drive back to Playa Santiago was the most welcome drive I've ever had. I wanted to go home.

Ray and the Russian, whose name I learned was Kitty, holed up in his hotel so he could write his articles. I went back to the boat, which had never felt so comfortable, and my normal routine of the coffee shop and Anna's Airstream, and Pirate's Cove and the beach. The beach was warm, the fishermen went out in the morning and came back every night, and the glorious and humble routines of life were back to normal. The seagulls still woke me up every morning, and yet a grim specter loomed over the town, that of Higgins Properties and their continuing demolition. Several empty spaces sat on the beachfront where historic cottages once had been, and I refrained from bothering Ray while he worked. He texted me a few times to assure me the first article was taking shape. Something this huge would need some close editorial attention and he couldn't afford to fuck anything up.

Things were obviously subdued at the Cove, especially with the sound of demolition all around us. It's hard to drink and have a good time while something special is being destroyed all around you. I just hoped that Ray was really writing that article, that the Russian prostitute wasn't distracting him, that his divorce wasn't distracting him. I would get occasional texts from him saying it was going well, he hadn't been this passionate about a project for a long time, that he was "in a good place." And then one night he wanted to meet me at the Cove.

He was there before me, with a big Pooka Pooka Bowl and a smile on his face.

"So?" I asked, sliding up to the bar. "How's what's her name?"

"Kitty? She's great. She makes me feel young, Aris. Young! Someday you'll understand that. But I have good news. My partner Jimmy Galvez at the *Times*, I told you about him, right? He wrote a piece for the paper two days ago, outlining some of the findings from those papers you sent us, and he got a call from the Attorney General's office. He had a long conversation with them, and I just sent them the first part of the piece I'm writing. It's going to be a series and I've just finished part one. They're looking at it, Jimmy sent them a copy of all those papers, and my piece will hit the *Times* tomorrow." He took a big sip of his drink. "Front page."

We drank to that. And the next day I checked out the article online. He'd interviewed a lot more people than I realized while he'd been here. The article detailed everything, from the murder to the bribing of the Santiago police, of at least two members of city council, one member of the Coastal Commission, one member of the water department. Money had passed hands; favors were given or promised. And in return this resort was pushed through on local and state levels. The investigation of the murder of Sam Bernard basically did not happen, thanks to the local police force, and the victim's ex-wife, a woman with no ties to the murder, was in custody awaiting trial. It was all there, on the cover of the *LA Times*, and there would be more.

The next day I went to the Cove and one of the old timers was outside, a retired groundskeeper for the college named Frank who was always at the bar.

"Did you hear?" he said when I approached.

"What??"

"Dave had a heart attack."

20

"He's in okay condition, I hear. But he wanted me to hang out here and tell people. He said his heart is only functioning at twenty percent. There's a bunch of liquid in there."

"Liquid?"

"Yeah, well, after his heart attack five years ago they told him to drink plenty of water, but he's drinking too much and not sweating it out enough…I don't know. He's pretty upset."

"When will he be back? Will he be okay?"

"He can't be on his feet all night long like he's been doing. And I don't think he can shake those drinks like he does. Basically from now on he's operating on twenty percent."

"What will happen to the bar? What will he do? I mean, no one else knows those recipes."

"Except Rogelio."

"Who?"

"Oh, you must not have met him. He was the other bartender. I guess he's the only one who knows the drinks."

"Who is he? Where is he?"

"Rogelio started as a barback and after Dave's dad died he started learning the drinks. He was good. But his dad got sick in Guadalajara and he's been back there ever since. I guess he left right before you came to town. Dave was saying they had a funeral, I think that was last week. And Dave has been paying Rogelio's family his usual salary ever since he's been gone. He has a wife and a son."

"Is he coming back?"

"Well, I think we all just wish the best for his family, and if and when he comes back, it will be at his own time. Certainly his family needs him in Guadalajara, what with the funeral and all that."

It was a week before Dave came back, and a few times the regulars just met on the beach outside the bar to mix drinks and hold a kind of vigil for him. When he came back he looked tired and he was only serving beers. In the meantime the demolition had stopped and we didn't know what was going on. Ray came by the boat to tell me he was going back to LA. I thanked him, but it was hard to explain all he'd done or how important it was to me. Kitty was with him, and I wished them both well.

It killed me to see Dave in his condition, a shell of his former self. A few times he made some drinks, but it winded him and he couldn't continue. They were sad days for me and I didn't know what to do.

And then one night I walked into the bar and something strange and magical was happening. I just stood at the entrance, not knowing what to think: a shorter, 40ish Mexican man was shaking drinks behind the bar. He was a serious man, with a small mustache. He wore a Hawaiian shirt. His shake was excellent and he was making the drinks with amazing swiftness and elegance. He rarely smiled, but there was a joyous sparkle in his eyes. A Mexican boy was running through the bar collecting empty glasses and stacking them in the washing bin in the corner. Dave was behind the bar, regaling the regulars with tales of yore, celebrities who had been in here, local characters who were long since gone. Here and there he made a drink or poured a beer or gave someone a bill. He was an elder statesman of the bar now. He'd passed into semi-retirement.

I walked out of the bar as I felt something well up inside me and my eyes began to water. Here was everything: I was finally seeing what it was all about. Life moved on, and things changed, but those very important things would be preserved somehow.

I finally went back inside and got a mai tai, and it was not the same mai tai that Dave would have made. The ingredients were the same, the recipe was the same, but it was Rogelio's mai tai. There was something unique in his shake, something in his proportions, his garnishes, that only he would do. And that's exactly how it should be. As I drank it I realized that it was a complex and unique work of art, unique to its maker, and that this bar would be okay. You couldn't destroy these drinks; they would live on somehow.

After I had a couple of drinks the bar emptied out a little, and it got quiet, and I looked up and saw Rogelio explaining the drinks in Spanish to his son. I made out a little of it, thanks to my

classes in high school, but he appeared to be telling the boy the
ı̄ tai and a zombie. The ingredients were different, the flavor was
both good, but one had to know the difference in order to appreciate

Some day Dave would be gone and Rogelio would own this place, and his son would be tending bar beside him, and there would be wonderful new drinks and new customers, and life would go on. I looked out at the beach, and felt the sea breeze come in, and I saw the waves rolling in and out. I was finally at peace.

21

The fallout was huge. Higgins Real Estate declared bankruptcy and half of their board was indicted. The lady from the Coastal Commission whom I'd met at the bar, she was indicted. Two city council members and the mayor were indicted. The police chief resigned and four police officers were indicted. The list went on, and it tore through Sacramento because it got pretty close to the governor, although nothing was ever proven. Psycho Billy disappeared, and his part of the story became a separate beast, since several state senators and a governor's aide had been going to his house for drugged out sex parties for years. We're talking bondage, Central American sex slaves, meth, cocaine, all the nasty stuff. None of this was connected to Higgins although Ray swears it was. He's still chasing down leads.

Grover Simpson came back. He'd been in Maui. It turned out that yes, the land was deeded to him, and he sued Higgins for damages as they were imploding. At his urging, the California Historical Conservation Society got involved and they began the process of protecting and restoring the historical properties in town, ensuring that it would never be turned into Downtown Disney. Red sold the Pirate's Cove building, and the adjacent parking lot, to Dave for two dollars and three mai tais. That's what Dave told me at least. I don't know how the mai tais were part of that, legally, but I like it.

Oh, Hilda Bernard: she was freed and sued the police for some enormous sum, in the eight figures I believe. Legal experts are saying she'll almost definitely get it. She and Eugene English started coming to the bar and everyone felt a little sheepish for so brazenly and casually accusing her of murder. I got to buy Eugene that drink I owed him and he's brought Anna and me back to the farm for steaks a couple of times.

22

The house was a 1920's craftsman about two blocks from the beach. It was classic beach cottage. The backyard was huge and overrun with weeds; for this place to be cool there would have to be a fire pit, maybe a hot tub, a barbecue, a bar. Then it would be the classic beach house. It's straight shot down 1ˢᵗ street to the sand. Anna and her mom walked through the house, oohing and ahhing.

"Three bedrooms," Anna said. "And a big kitchen. It's perfect for a family or as a weekend vacation house."

Anna's mom stood in the kitchen, looking out the window at the backyard. "Aristotle, if you rent it out as a weekend getaway, you can always come stay here when it's not booked. My friend can handle all of that for you, too. She does all the booking, the cleaning, the maintenance. If you rent it out for eight or ten days a month it'll pay the mortgage."

"The price is pretty amazing, right mom?" said Anna. "I mean, 250 – now is the time to buy."

"Or I could just find a family to rent it to," I said. "Like a professor at the college or something. I could see a nice professor and his family living here. This could be his study," I gestured at one of the bedrooms. "Where he plans his lectures."

I was lost in thought.

"Maybe we should make an offer," I said, and Anna's mom's face beamed. Not a bad idea, to sit around and get free money every month. I wouldn't mind that at all.

Later, when Anna's mom had gone to her office to make the offer and we had nothing to do but sit around and wait to hear back from the seller, I asked Anna if I could buy her a drink. We walked through town to the Cove and I asked her what we were supposed to do now.

"What do you mean?"

"Well, without any mystery to solve, what do we do next?"

She shrugged. "Build equity?"

At the bar the atmosphere was perfect. A chilly wind blew in off the ocean and the seagulls were making a ruckus, and the Getz/Gilberto album was playing. Building equity wasn't quite what I was looking for. I mean, it was a good thing to do, and I was all for it, but I needed adventure. I wanted new horizons. There was an old, old tattered map of America on the wall amongst all the other kitschy stuff.

"Look," I pointed at the Grand Canyon. "I've never been here. Have you? And the last time I was at Yosemite was when I was twelve. And I've heard that Santa Fe is amazing."

"We could take the Airstream and see America," she said.

"Might be a good idea."

We spent the rest of the night planning out a route. The other regulars started helping us, and pretty soon they'd given us a list of places that we had to go. The route was a pretty good one. We had to find the next mystery. Somewhere out there it was waiting for us.

Made in the USA
San Bernardino, CA
11 December 2016